Quiz# 87180

CIRQUE DU FREAK
THE SAGA OF DARREN SHAN

Killers of
the Dawn

Rave reviews for the CIRQUE DU FREAK series

Over 1.5 million copies sold!

The *New York Times* bestselling series

"Fast-paced and compelling, full of satisfying macabre touches—*Cirque Du Freak* explores the powerful fascination of the dangerous and unnatural and also, movingly, the obligations of friendship."
— J. K. Rowling

"The Saga of Darren Shan is poised to capture a wide audience of series horror readers." — *Publishers Weekly*

"Gross-out horror fans will devour it and clamor for the next in the series." — *Kirkus*

"Chockful of wonderfully inventive details." — *Booklist*

"Shan creates heart-pounding, page-turning action that will keep readers reading." — *School Library Journal*

"For those fans of *Buffy* and *Angel*, here is another book to satisfy their vampiric tastes." — *VOYA*

Book 9

CIRQUE DU FREAK
THE SAGA OF DARREN SHAN

Killers of
the Dawn

by Darren Shan

LITTLE, BROWN AND COMPANY
New York ᪲ Boston

Little, Brown and Company

Hachette Book Group USA
237 Park Avenue, New York, NY 10017
Visit our Web site at www.lb-teens.com

First U.S. Mass Market Edition: September 2006

The characters and events portrayed in this book are fictitious.
Any similarity to real persons, living or dead, is coincidental
and not intended by the author.

First published in Great Britain by Collins in 2002

Library of Congress Cataloging-in-Publication Data

Shan, Darren.
    Killers of the dawn / by Darren Shan. — 1st U.S. ed.
        p.   cm. — (The saga of Darren Shan ; bk. 9)
    Summary: As his battles against the vampanze continue, Darren
Shan is framed as public enemy number one.
    ISBN-10: 0-316-10666-7 / ISBN-13: 978-0-316-10666-7
    [1. Vampires — Fiction. 2. Horror stories.]   I. Title: At head of
title: Cirque Du Freak. II. Title.
PZ7.S52823Ki 2005
[Fic] — dc22   2004044158

10 9 8 7 6 5 4 3

Q-BF

Printed in the United States of America

Also in the Cirque Du Freak Series:

Cirque Du Freak (Book 1)
The Vampire's Assistant (Book 2)
Tunnels of Blood (Book 3)
Vampire Mountain (Book 4)
Trials of Death (Book 5)
The Vampire Prince (Book 6)
Hunters of the Dusk (Book 7)
Allies of the Night (Book 8)
The Lake of Souls (Book 10)
The Lord of the Shadows (Book 11)
Sons of Destiny (Book 12)

For:

Bas—my dawn bird

OBE (Order of the Bloody Entrails) to:
Maiko "minder" Enomoto
&
Megumi "fault-finder" Hashimoto
Gillie Russell & Zoë Clarke—the Sisters Grimm
The Christopher Little Clan—troll-masters

PROLOGUE

IT WAS AN AGE of deceit. Everyone was suspicious of everyone else — and with good reason! You never knew when a trusted ally would turn, bare his fangs, and rip you to pieces.

The vampires and vampaneze were at war — the War of the Scars — and the result hinged upon finding and killing the Lord of the Vampaneze. If the vampires did that, victory would be theirs. Otherwise, the night would belong to their purple-skinned blood-cousins, who would drive the vampires to extinction.

Three vampires were sent by Mr. Desmond Tiny to hunt the Vampaneze Lord — Vancha March, Larten Crepsley, and me, Darren Shan. I'm a half-vampire.

Mr. Tiny told us that other vampires couldn't assist us in our hunt, but non-vampires could. Thus, the only one to accompany us was a Little Person called Harkat

Mulds, though a witch known as Lady Evanna also traveled with us for a short time during our quest.

After unwittingly letting the Vampaneze Lord slip through our fingers in the first of four predicted encounters, we traveled to the city of Mr. Crepsley's birth. We didn't expect to find the Lord of the Vampaneze there — we came to track down and stop a gang of vampaneze who were murdering humans.

We attracted two more companions in the city — my ex-girlfriend, Debbie Hemlock, and Steve Leopard. Steve used to be my best friend. He said he'd become a vampaneze-hunter, and swore he'd help us put an end to the killer vampaneze. Mr. Crepsley was suspicious of Steve — he believed Steve had evil blood — but I persuaded him to grant my old friend the benefit of the doubt.

Our target was an insane, hook-handed vampaneze. It turned out he was another of my ex-associates — R.V., which originally stood for Reggie Veggie, though he now claimed it was short for Righteous Vampaneze. He was once an eco-warrior, until his hands had been bitten off by the Wolf-Man at the Cirque Du Freak. He blamed me for the accident, and had teamed up with the vampaneze in order to exact revenge.

We could have killed R.V., but we knew he was in

league with other vampaneze, and we chose instead to trick him into leading us to them. What we didn't know was that we were actually the flies in the trap, not the spiders. Deep beneath the streets of the city, dozens of vampaneze were waiting for us. Among them stood the Lord of the Vampaneze and his protector, Gannen Harst — Vancha March's estranged brother.

In an underground cavern, Steve Leopard revealed his true colors. He was a half-vampaneze and had plotted with R.V. and the Vampaneze Lord to lure us to our doom. But Steve underestimated us, and I overcame him and would have killed him — except R.V. captured Debbie and threatened to murder her in retaliation.

While this was happening, my allies pursued the Vampaneze Lord, but the odds were stacked against them and he escaped. The vampaneze could have slaughtered us all, but we would have killed many of them in the process. To avoid the bloodshed, Gannen Harst let us go and gave us a fifteen-minute head start — it would be easier for the vampaneze to kill us in the tunnels.

With me holding Steve Leopard hostage, and Vancha clutching a vampet — a human who'd been trained in the ways of the vampaneze — we retreated, leaving R.V. free to do all the terrible things he wanted to Debbie. Through the tunnels we hurried, exhausted and distraught, knowing the vampaneze would soon swarm after us and cut us down dead if they caught up. . . .

CHAPTER ONE

WE SCURRIED through the tunnels, Mr. Crepsley leading the way, Vancha and I in the middle with our prisoners, Harkat bringing up the rear. We said as little as possible, and I cuffed Steve into silence whenever he started to speak — I wasn't in the mood to listen to his threats or insults.

I didn't have a watch, but I'd been ticking off the seconds inside my head. About ten minutes or so had passed by my reckoning. We'd moved out of the modern tunnels and were back in the warren of old, damp tunnels. There was still a long way to go — plenty of time for the vampaneze to run us down.

We came to a junction and Mr. Crepsley took the left turn. Vancha started to follow him, then stopped. "Larten," he called him back. When Mr. Crepsley returned, Vancha crouched low. He was almost invisible in the darkness of the tunnels. "We have to try and shake them off," he said. "If we make straight for the surface, they'll be upon us before we're halfway there."

"But we could lose ourselves if we detour," Mr. Crepsley said. "We do not know this area. We might run into a dead end."

"Aye," Vancha sighed, "but it's a chance we'll have to take. I'll act as a decoy and go back the way we came. The rest of you try and find an alternative route out. I'll work my way back to you later, if the luck of the vampires is with me."

Mr. Crepsley thought about that a moment, then nodded quickly. "Luck, Sire," he said, but Vancha was already gone, disappearing into the gloom in an instant, moving with the almost perfect silence of the vampires.

We rested a moment, than took the right tunnel and pressed on, Harkat now in charge of the vampet Vancha had kidnapped. We moved quickly but carefully, trying not to leave any signs that we'd passed this way. At the end of the tunnel, we branched off, again to the right. As we entered a fresh stretch of tunnel, Steve coughed loudly. Mr. Crepsley was on him in a flash. "Do that again and you die!" he snapped, and I sensed the blade of his knife pressing against Steve's throat.

"It was a real cough — not a signal," Steve snarled in reply.

"It matters not!" Mr. Crepsley hissed. "The next time, I will kill you."

Steve was silent after that, as was the vampet. We marched steadily upward, instinctively navigating the tunnels, wading through water and waste. I felt terrible, tired and drawn, but I didn't slow down. It must be daylight above ground, or very close to it. Our only hope was to get clear of the tunnels before the vampaneze found us — the sunlight should prevent them from pursuing us any further.

A short while later, we heard the vampaneze and vampets. They were coming up the tunnels at great speed, not having to worry about stealth. Mr. Crepsley dropped back a bit, to check if they were following us, but they didn't seem to have found our trail — all of them appeared to have gone after Vancha.

We continued to climb, working our way closer to the surface. Our pursuers kept passing in and out of earshot. By the sounds they made, they'd realized we weren't following the shortest route back, and had stopped and fanned out in search of us. I guessed that we were at least half an hour from ground level. If they located us anytime soon, we were certainly doomed. The tunnels were as tight as they were dark — a lone, well-placed vampet would have no difficulty mowing us down with a rifle or arrow-gun.

We were picking our way over a heap of rubble in a crumbling tunnel when we were eventually spotted. A vampet with a torch entered the tunnel at the far end, picked us out with a strong beam of light, and roared triumphantly. "I've found them! They're here! They —"

He got no further. A figure stepped out of the shadows behind him, grabbed his head and twisted sharply, left then right. The vampet dropped to the ground. His assailant paused just long enough to turn off the torch, then hurried over. I knew without having to see him that it was Vancha.

"Good timing," Harkat muttered as the scraggly Prince joined us.

"I've been shadowing you for a while," Vancha said. "He's not the first one I've picked off. He just got a bit closer to you than the others."

"Any idea how far we are from the surface?" I asked.

"No," Vancha said. "I was ahead of you earlier, but I've been bringing up the rear for the last quarter of an hour, covering you and laying a few false trails."

"What about the vampaneze?" Mr. Crepsley said. "Are they close?"

"Aye," came Vancha's reply, and then he slipped away again, to provide more cover.

Slightly further ahead, we found ourselves in familiar tunnels. We'd explored a vast slice of the city's infrastructure when hunting for the vampaneze, and had been in this section three or four times. We were no more than six or seven minutes from safety. Mr. Crepsley whistled loudly, signaling to Vancha. The Prince swiftly joined us and we pushed on vigorously, finding a new lease on life.

"There they go!"

The shout came from a tunnel to our left. We didn't stop to check how many were nearby — putting our heads down, we pushed Steve and the vampet in front and ran.

The vampaneze weren't long surging after us. Vancha dropped back and kept them at bay with his shurikens — sharp, multi-edged throwing stars that were lethal when thrown by one as experienced as Vancha March. By the hysterical voices, I knew most — if not all — of the vampaneze and vampets had now converged behind us, but the tunnel we were in ran straight ahead, with hardly any side-tunnels opening out of it. Our enemies weren't able to sneak around and attack us from the side or in front — they were forced to follow behind.

As we got closer to street level, the tunnels grew brighter, and my half-vampire eyes quickly adjusted to the dim light. I was now able to see the vampaneze and vampets trailing behind — and they were able to see us! The vampaneze, like vampires, had sworn not to use any missile-firing weapons such as guns or bows, but the vampets weren't limited by that oath. They began firing as soon as they had a clear line of sight, and we had to run doubled-over. If we'd had to cover a long distance in that uncomfortable crouch, they'd have surely picked us off one by one, but within a minute of them opening fire, we arrived at a steel ladder leading up to a manhole.

"Go!" Vancha barked, unleashing a hail of shurikens at the vampets.

Mr. Crepsley grabbed me and shoved me up the ladder. I didn't protest at being first. It made the most sense — if the vampaneze pressed forward, Mr. Crepsley was better equipped to fight them off.

At the top of the ladder I braced myself, then heaved against the manhole cover with my shoulders. It flew off, clearing the way up. I hauled myself out and quickly checked my surroundings. I was in the middle of a small street; it was early in the morning and nobody was about. Leaning back over the manhole, I yelled, "It's clear!"

Seconds later, Steve Leopard crawled out of the manhole, grimacing in the sunlight (almost blinding after being down the tunnels so long). Then Harkat came, followed by the vampet. There was a short delay after that. The tunnel underneath echoed with angry gun retorts. Fearing the worst, I was about to climb back down the ladder to check on Mr. Crepsley and Vancha when the orange-haired vampire burst out of the manhole, gasping wildly. Almost immediately, Vancha shot out after him. The pair must have jumped, one directly after the other.

As soon as Vancha was clear of the manhole, I stumbled across the street, picked up the cover, shuffled back with it and set it in place. Then all four of us gathered around it, Vancha grasping several shurikens, Mr. Crepsley his knives, Harket his axe, and me my sword. We waited ten seconds. Twenty. Half a minute. A minute passed. Mr. Crepsley and Vancha were sweating stingingly beneath the wan glare of the morning sun.

Nobody came.

Vancha cocked an eyebrow at Mr. Crepsley. "Think they've given up?"

"For a moment." Mr. Crepsley nodded, backing off warily, switching his attention to Steve and the vampet, making sure they didn't make a break for freedom.

"We should get out of . . . this city," Harkat said, wiping a layer of dried blood from around his stitched-together grey face. Like Mr. Crepsley and Vancha, he was nicked in many places after his battle with the vampaneze, but the cuts weren't serious. "It would be suicide to remain."

"Run, rabbits, run," Steve murmured, and I cuffed him around the ears again, shutting him up.

"I'm not leaving Debbie," I said. "R.V.'s a crazed killer. I'm not going to abandon her to him."

"What did you do to that maniac to madden him so much?" Vancha asked, peeking down one of the small holes in the manhole cover, still not entirely convinced that we were in the clear. The purple animal hides he dressed in were hanging from his frame in shreds, and his dyed green hair was flecked with blood.

"Nothing," I sighed. "There was an accident at the Cirque Du Freak. He —"

"We have no time for recollections," Mr. Crepsley interrupted, tearing off the left sleeve of his red shirt, which had been slashed in as many places as Vancha's hides. He squinted up at the sun. "In our state, we cannot bear to stay in the sun very long. Whatever our choice, we must choose soon."

"Darren's right," Vancha said. "We can't leave. Not because of Debbie — much as I like her, I wouldn't sacrifice myself for her — but the Lord of the

Vampaneze. We know he's down there. We have to go after him."

"But he's too well protected," Harkat protested. "Those tunnels are full of vampaneze . . . and vampets. We'd perish for certain if we went . . . down again. I say we flee and come back . . . later, with help."

"You've forgotten Mr. Tiny's warning," Vancha said. "We can't ask other vampires for help. I don't care how poor the odds are — we must try to breach their defenses and kill their Lord."

"I agree," Mr. Crepsley said. "But now is not the time. We are wounded and exhausted. We should rest and form a plan of action. The question is, where do we retire to — the apartments we have been using, or elsewhere?"

"Elsewhere," Harkat said instantly. "The vampaneze know where . . . we've been living. If we stay, we'd be crazy to go where . . . they can attack anytime they like."

"I don't know," I muttered. "It was weird, the way they let us leave. I know Gannen said it was to spare the lives of his companions, but if they'd killed us, they were guaranteed victory in the War of the Scars. I think there's more to it than he was letting on. Having spared us when they had us trapped on their own turf, I doubt they'll come all the way up here to fight on our territory."

My companions mused on that in silence.

"I think we should return to our base and try to make sense of this," I said. "Even if we can't, we can get some rest and tend to our wounds. Then, come night, we'll attack."

"Sounds good to me," Vancha said.

"As good a plan as any," Mr. Crepsley sighed.

"Harkat?" I asked the Little Person.

His round green eyes were full of doubt, but he grimaced and nodded. "I think we're fools to stay, but if . . . we're going to, I guess at least we have weapons and . . . provisions there."

"Besides," Vancha added grimly, "most of the apartments are empty. It's quiet." He ran a menacing finger along the neck of his captured vampet, a shaven-headed man with the dark "V" of the vampets tattooed above either ear. "There are some questions I want answered, but the asking won't be pleasant. It'll be for the best if there's nobody around to hear."

The vampet sneered at Vancha as though unimpressed, but I could see fear in his blood-rimmed eyes. Vampaneze had the strength to withstand horrible torture, but vampets were human. A vampire could do terrible things to a human.

Mr. Crepsley and Vancha wrapped their robes and hides around their heads and shoulders, to protect them from the worst of the sun. Then, pushing Steve and the vampet ahead of us, we climbed to roof level, got our bearings, and wearily headed for base.

CHAPTER TWO

"BASE" WAS THE FIFTH FLOOR of an ancient, largely abandoned block of apartments. It was where Steve had set up camp. We'd moved in when we teamed up with him. We occupied three apartments on the floor. While Mr. Crepsley, Harkat, and I bundled Steve into the middle apartment, Vancha grabbed the vampet by his ears and hauled him off to the apartment on the right.

"Will he torture him?" I asked Mr. Crepsley, pausing at the door.

"Yes," the vampire answered bluntly.

I didn't like the thought of that, but the circumstances called for swift, true answers. Vancha was only doing what had to be done. In war there's sometimes no room for compassion or humanity.

Entering our apartment, I hurried to the fridge. It

didn't work — the apartment had no electricity — but we stored our drinks and food there.

"Anyone hungry or thirsty?" I asked.

"I'll have a *steak* — extra bloody — fries, and a Coke to go," Steve quipped. He'd made himself comfortable on the couch, and was smiling around at us as though we were one big happy family.

I ignored him. "Mr. Crepsley? Harkat?"

"Water, please," Mr. Crepsley said, shrugging off his tattered red cloak so he could examine his wounds. "And bandages," he added.

"Are you hurt?" Harkat asked.

"Not really. But the tunnels we crawled through were unhygienic. We should all clean out our wounds to prevent infection."

I washed my hands, then threw some food together. I wasn't hungry but I felt I should eat — my body was working solely on excess adrenaline; it needed feeding. Harkat and Mr. Crepsley also laid into the food and soon we were finishing off the last of the crumbs.

We offered none to Steve.

While we were tending to our wounds, I stared hatefully at Steve, who grinned back mockingly. "How long did it take to set this up?" I asked. "Getting us here, arranging those false papers for me and sending me to school, luring us down the tunnels — how long?"

"Years," Steve replied proudly. "It wasn't easy. You don't know the half of it. That cavern where the trap was set — we built that from scratch, along with the tunnels leading in and out of it. We built other caverns too. There's one I'm especially proud of. I hope I have the chance to show it to you some time."

"You went to all this trouble just for us?" Mr. Crepsley asked, startled.

"Yes," Steve replied smugly.

"Why?" I asked. "Wouldn't it have been easier to fight us in the old, existing tunnels?"

"Easier," Steve agreed, "but not as much fun. I've developed a love of the dramatic over the years — a bit like Mr. Tiny. You should appreciate that, having worked for a circus for so long."

"What I don't understand," Harkat mused, "is what the . . . Vampaneze Lord was doing there, or why the other vampaneze . . . aided you in your insane plans."

"Not as insane as you might think," Steve retorted. "The Vampaneze Lord knew you'd be coming. Mr. Tiny told him all about the hunters who would dog his footsteps. He also said that running away or hiding wasn't an option — if our Lord didn't make a stand and face those who hunted him, the War of the Scars would be lost.

"When he learned of my interest in you — and R.V.'s — he consulted us and together we hatched this plan. Gannen Harst cautioned against it — he's old school and would have preferred a direct confrontation — but the Vampaneze Lord shares my theatrical tastes."

"This Lord of yours," Mr. Crepsley said. "What does he look like?"

Steve laughed and shook a finger at the vampire. "Now, now, Larten. You don't honestly expect me to describe him, do you? He's been very careful not to show his face, even to most of those who follow him."

"We could torture it out of you," I growled.

"I doubt it," Steve smirked. "I'm half-vampaneze. I can take anything you can dish out. I'd let you kill me before I betrayed the clan." He shrugged off the heavy jacket he'd been wearing since we met. Strong chemical odors wafted off him.

"He's not shivering anymore," Harkat said suddenly. Steve had told us he suffered from colds, which was why he had to wear lots of clothes and smear on lotions to protect himself.

"Of course not," Steve said. "That was all for show."

"You have the slyness of a demon," Mr. Crepsley grunted. "By claiming to be susceptible to colds, you were able to wear gloves to hide your fingertip scars, and douse yourself in sickly-smelling lotions to mask your vampaneze stench."

"The smell was the difficult bit," Steve laughed. "I knew your sensitive noses would sniff my blood out, so I had to distract them." He pulled a face. "But it hasn't been easy. My sense of smell is also highly developed, so the fumes have played havoc with my sinuses. The headaches are awful."

"My heart bleeds for you," I snarled sarcastically, and Steve laughed with delight. He was having a great time, even though he was our prisoner. His eyes were alight with evil glee.

"You won't be grinning if R.V. refuses to trade Debbie for you," I told him.

"True enough," he admitted. "But I live only to see you and Creepy Crepsley suffer. I could die happy knowing the torment you'll endure if R.V. carves up your darling teacher girlfriend."

I shook my head, appalled. "How did you get so twisted?" I asked. "We were friends, almost like brothers. You weren't evil then. What happened to you?"

Steve's face darkened. "I was betrayed," he said quietly.

"That isn't true," I replied. "I saved your life. I gave up everything so that you could live. I didn't want to become a half-vampire. I —"

"Shut it!" Steve snapped. "Torture me if you wish, but don't insult me with lies. I know you plotted with

Creepy Crepsley to spite me. I could have been a vampire, powerful, long-living, majestic. But you left me as a human, to shuffle through a pitifully short life, weak and afraid like everybody else. Well, guess what? I outsmarted you! I tracked down those in the other camp and gained my rightful powers and privileges anyway!"

"For all the good it has done you," Mr. Crepsley snorted.

"What do you mean?" Steve snapped.

"You have wasted your life on hatred and revenge," Mr. Crepsley said. "What good is life if there is no joy or creative purpose? You would have been better off living five years as a human than five hundred as a monster."

"I'm no monster!" Steve snarled. "I'm . . ." He stopped and growled something to himself. "Enough of this crap," he declared aloud. "You're boring me. If you haven't anything more intelligent to say, keep your mouths shut."

"Impudent cur!" Mr. Crepsley roared, and swung the back of his hand across Steve's cheek, drawing blood. Steve sneered at the vampire, wiped the blood off with his fingers, then put them to his lips.

"One night soon, it'll be *your* blood I dine on," he whispered, then lapsed into silence.

Exasperated and weary, Mr. Crepsley, Harkat, and

I also fell silent. We finished cleaning our wounds, then lay back and relaxed. If we'd been alone, we'd have dozed off — but none of us dared shut our eyes with a destructive beast like Steve Leopard in the room.

More than an hour after Vancha had taken his captive vampet aside, he returned. His face was dark and although he'd washed his hands before coming in, he hadn't been able to remove all the traces of blood. Some of it was his own, from wounds received in the tunnels, but most had come from the vampet.

Vancha found a bottle of warm beer in the out-of-order fridge, yanked the top off and downed it hungrily. He normally never drank anything other than fresh water, milk, and blood — but these were hardly normal times.

He wiped around his mouth with the back of a hand when he was done, then stared at the faint red stains on his flesh. "He was a brave man," Vancha said quietly. "He resisted longer than I thought possible. I had to do bad things to make him talk. I . . ." He shivered and opened another bottle. There were bitter tears in his eyes as he drank.

"Is he dead?" I asked, my voice trembling.

Vancha sighed and looked away. "We're at war. We cannot afford to spare our enemies' lives. Besides, by the time I'd finished, it seemed cruel to let him live. Killing him was a mercy in the end."

"Praise the gods of the vampires for small mercies," Steve laughed, then flinched as Vancha spun, drew a shuriken, and sent it flying at him. The sharp throwing star buried itself in the material of the couch, less than half an inch beneath Steve's right ear.

"I won't miss with the next," Vancha swore, and at last the smile slipped from Steve's face, as he realized how serious the Prince was.

Mr. Crepsley got up and laid a calming hand on Vancha's shoulder, directing him to a chair. "Was the interrogation worthwhile?" he asked. "Had the vampet anything new to reveal?"

Vancha didn't answer immediately. He was still glaring at Steve. Then the question sunk in and he wiped around his large eyes with the ends of one of his animal hides. "He'd plenty to say," Vancha grunted, then lapsed into silence and stared down at the bottle of beer in his hands, as though he didn't know how it got there.

"The vampet!" he said loudly after a minute of quiet, head snapping up, eyes clicking into focus. "Yes. I found out, for starters, why Gannen didn't kill us, and why the others fought so cagily." Leaning forward, he lobbed the empty beer bottle at Steve, who swatted it aside, then stared arrogantly back at the Prince. "Only the Vampaneze Lord can kill us," Vancha said softly.

"What do you mean?" I frowned.

"He's bound by Mr. Tiny's rules, the same as us," Vancha explained. "Just as *we* can't call upon others for help in tracking and fighting him, *he* can't ask his underlings to kill us. Mr. Tiny said he had to kill us himself to ensure victory. He can call upon all the vampaneze he likes to fight us, but if one should strike too deeply and inflict a fatal wound, they're destined to lose the war."

That was exciting news and we discussed it eagerly. Until now, we thought we stood no chance against the Vampaneze Lord's minions — there were simply too many of them for us to cut a path through. But if they weren't allowed to kill us . . .

"Let's not get carried away," Harkat cautioned. "Even if they can't kill us, they can . . . stall and subdue us. If they capture us and give us to . . . their Lord, it will be a simple matter for him to . . . drive a stake through our hearts."

"How come they didn't kill *you*?" I asked Harkat. "You're not one of the three hunters."

"Maybe they don't know that," Harkat said.

Steve muttered something beneath his breath.

"What was that?" Vancha shouted, prodding him sharply with his left foot.

"I said we didn't know before, but we do now!" Steve jeered. "At least," he added sulkily, "*I* know."

"You did not know who the hunters were?" Mr. Crepsley asked.

Steve shook his head. "We knew there were three of you, and Mr. Tiny told us that one would be a child, so we had Darren pegged straight off. But when five of you turned up — you three, Harkat and Debbie — we weren't sure about the others. We guessed the hunters would be vampires, but we didn't want to take unnecessary chances."

"Is that why you pretended to be our ally?" I asked. "You wanted to get close to us, to figure out who the hunters were?"

"That was part of it." Steve nodded. "Although mostly I just wanted to toy with you. It was fun, getting so close that I could kill you whenever I wished, delaying the fatal blow until the time was right."

"He's a fool," Vancha snorted. "Anyone who wouldn't strike his foe dead at the first opportunity is asking for trouble."

"Steve Leonard is many things," Mr. Crepsley said, "but not foolish." He rubbed the long scar on the left side of his face, thinking deeply. "You thought this plan through most thoroughly, did you not?" he asked Steve.

"I sure did," Steve smirked.

"You accounted for every possible twist and turn?"

"As many as I could imagine."

Mr. Crepsley stopped stroking his scar and his eyes narrowed. "Then you must have considered what would happen if we escaped."

Steve's smile widened but he said nothing.

"What was the backup plan?" Mr. Crepsley asked, his voice strained.

"'Backup plan'?" Steve echoed innocently.

"Do not play games with me!" Mr. Crepsley hissed. "You must have discussed alternate plans with R.V. and Gannen Harst. Once you had revealed your location to us, you could not afford to sit back and wait. Time is precious now that we know where your Lord is hiding, and how those with him cannot take our lives."

Mr. Crepsley stopped speaking and snapped to his feet. Vancha was only a second behind him. Their eyes locked and, as one, they exclaimed, "A trap!"

"I knew he came too quietly up the tunnels," Vancha growled, hurrying to the apartment door, opening it, and checking the corridor outside. "Deserted."

"I will try the window," Mr. Crepsley said, starting toward it.

"No point," Vancha said. "Vampaneze wouldn't attack in the open by day."

"No," Mr. Crepsley agreed, "but vampets would." He reached the window and drew back the heavy blind which was blocking the harmful rays of the sun. His breath caught in his throat. "Charna's guts!" he gasped.

Vancha, Harkat, and I rushed over to see what had upset him (Vancha grabbed hold of Steve on the way). What we saw caused us all to curse, except Steve, who laughed deliriously.

The street outside was teeming with police cars, army vans, policemen, and soldiers. They were lined up in front of the building, and stretched around the sides. Many carried rifles. In the building opposite, we glimpsed figures in the windows, also armed. As we watched, a helicopter buzzed down from overhead and hung in the air a couple of floors above us. There was a soldier in the helicopter with a rifle so big it could have been used to shoot elephants.

But the marksman wasn't interested in elephants. He was aiming at the same target as those in the building and on the ground — *us!*

CHAPTER THREE

As a strong spotlight was trained on the window to dazzle us, we all turned to one side and let the blind fall back into place. Retreating, Vancha cursed at his loudest and vilest, while the rest of us glanced uneasily at one another, waiting for someone to propose a plan.

"How did they sneak up without . . . us hearing?" Harkat asked.

"We weren't paying attention to what was happening outside," I said.

"Even so," Harkat insisted, "we should have . . . picked up on the sirens."

"They didn't use sirens," Steve laughed. "They were warned to tread quietly. And, before you waste time checking, they've got the rear of the building and roof covered as well as the front." As we stared at him questioningly, he said, "I wasn't distracted. *I* heard them coming."

Vancha bellowed madly at Steve, then made a dive for him. Mr. Crepsley stepped into his path to reason with him, but Vancha shoved him aside without regard and charged towards Steve, murder in his eyes.

A voice from outside, amplified by a megaphone, stopped him.

"You in there!" it bellowed. *"Killers!"*

Vancha hesitated, fingers balled into fists, then pointed at Steve and snarled, "Later!" Spinning, he hurried to the window and nudged the blind aside a fraction. Light from the sun and spotlight flooded the room.

Letting the blind fall back into place, Vancha roared, "Turn off the light!"

"No chance!" the person with the megaphone laughed in reply.

Vancha stood there a moment, thinking, then nodded at Mr. Crepsley and Harkat. "Check the corridors above and below. Find out if they're inside the building. Don't clash with them—if that lot outside start firing, they'll cut us to ribbons."

Mr. Crepsley and Harkat obeyed without question.

"Bring that sorry excuse for a dog over here," Vancha said to me, and I dragged Steve to the window.

Vancha wrapped a hand around Steve's throat and growled in his ear, "Why are they here?"

"They think you're the killers," Steve chuckled. "The ones who killed all those humans."

"You son of a mongrel!" Vancha snarled.

"Please," Steve replied smugly. "Let's not get personal."

Mr. Crepsley and Harkat returned.

"They're packed tight two . . . above," Harkat reported.

"The same two floors below," Mr. Crepsley said grimly.

Vancha cursed again, then thought quickly. "We'll break through the floorboards," he decided. "The humans will be in the halls. They won't expect us to go straight down through the apartments."

"Yes they will," Steve disagreed. "They've been warned to fill every room below, above and adjoining."

Vancha stared at Steve, looking for the slightest hint of a bluff. When he found none, his features softened and the ghostly traces of defeat welled in his eyes. Then he shook his head and put self-pity behind him.

"We have to talk to them," he said. "Find out where we stand and maybe buy some time to think this through. Anyone want to volunteer?" When nobody replied, he grunted. "Guess that means I'm the negotiator. Just don't blame me if it all goes wrong." Leaving the blind over the window, he smashed a pane of glass, then leant close and shouted at the humans below. "Who's down there and what the hell do you want?"

There was a pause, then the same voice as before spoke to us via a megaphone. "Who am I talking to?" the person asked. Now that I concentrated on the voice, I realized it was a woman's.

"None of your business!" Vancha roared.

Another pause. Then, "We knew your names. Larten Crepsley, Vancha March, Darren Shan, and Harkat Mulds. I just want to know which one of you I'm in contact with."

Vancha's jaw dropped.

Steve doubled over with laughter.

"Tell them who you are," Harkat whispered. "They know too much. Best to act like we're . . . cooperating."

Vancha nodded, then shouted through the covered hole in the window, "Vancha March."

As he did that, I peeked through a gap at the side of the blind, looking for weak points in the defenses below. I didn't find any, but I did get a fix on the woman who was speaking to us — tall and broad, with short white hair.

"Listen, March," the woman called as I stepped away from the window. "I'm Chief Inspector Alice Burgess. I'm running this freak show." An ironic choice of words, though none of us commented on it. "If you want to negotiate a deal, you'll be negotiating with me. One warning — I'm not here to play games. I've more than two hundred men and women out here and inside your building, just dying to put a round of bullets through your black excuse for a heart. At the first sign that you're messing with us, I'll give the order and they'll open fire. Understand?"

Vancha bared his teeth and snarled, "I understand." Then he repeated it, louder, so she could hear. "I understand!"

"Good," Chief Inspector Burgess responded. "First of all — are your hostages alive and unharmed?"

"'Hostages'?" Vancha replied.

"Steve Leonard and Mark Ryter. We know you have them, so don't act the innocent."

"Mark Ryter must have been the vampet," I remarked.

"You're soooooo observant," Steve laughed, then pushed Vancha aside and put his face up close to the window. "This is Steve Leonard!" he yelled, mimicking terror. "They haven't killed me yet, but they killed Mark. They tortured him first. It was horrible. They —"

He stopped, as though we'd cut him off mid-sentence, and stepped back, taking a self-indulgent bow.

"Sons of . . ." the officer cursed over the megaphone, then collected her wits and addressed us calmly and dryly. "OK — this is how it works. Release your remaining hostage. When he's safely in our custody, come down after him, one at a time. Any sign of a weapon, or any unexpected moves, and you're history."

"Let's talk about this," Vancha shouted.

"No talking," Burgess snapped.

"We're not going to release him," Vancha roared. "You don't know what he is, what he's done. Let me —"

A rifle fired and a volley of bullets tore up the outside of the building. We fell to the floor, cursing and yelping, although there was no cause for concern — the marksmen were aiming deliberately high.

When the scream of bullets died away, the Chief Inspector addressed us again. "That was a warning — your last. Next time we shoot to kill. No bargaining. No trade-offs. No talking. You've terrorized this city for most of a year, but it stops here. You're through.

"Two minutes," she said. "Then we come in after you."

A troubled silence descended.

"That's that," Harkat muttered after a handful of slow-ticking seconds. "We're finished."

"Maybe," Vancha sighed. Then his gaze fell on Steve and he grinned. "But we won't die alone."

Vancha brought the fingers of his right hand together and held them out straight so they formed a blade of flesh and bone. He raised the hand above his head like a knife and advanced.

Steve closed his eyes and waited for death with a smile on his face.

"Wait," Mr. Crepsley said softly, halting him. "There *is* a way out."

Vancha paused. "How?" he asked suspiciously.

"The window," Mr. Crepsley said. "We jump. They will not expect that."

Vancha considered the plan. "The drop's no problem," he mused. "Not for us, anyway. How about you, Harkat?"

"Five stories?" Harkat smiled. "I could do that . . . in my sleep."

"But what do we do once down there?" Vancha asked. "The place is crawling with police and soldiers."

"We flit," Mr. Crepsley said. "I will carry Darren. You carry Harkat. It will not be easy — they might shoot us before we can work up to flitting speed — but it can be done. With luck."

"It's crazy," Vancha growled, then winked at us. "I like it!" He pointed at Steve. "But we kill him before we leave."

"One minute!" Alice Burgess shouted through her megaphone.

Steve hadn't moved. His eyes were still closed. He was still smiling.

I didn't want Vancha to kill Steve. Although he'd betrayed us, he'd been my friend once, and the thought of him being killed in cold blood disturbed me. Also, there was Debbie to think about — if we killed Steve, R.V. would certainly kill Debbie in retaliation. It was crazy to worry about her, considering the trouble we were in, but I couldn't help it.

I was about to ask Vancha to spare Steve's life — although I didn't think he'd listen to me — when Mr. Crepsley beat me to the punch.

"We cannot kill him," he said, sounding disgusted.

"Come again?" Vancha blinked.

"It is not the end of the world if we are captured," Mr. Crepsley said.

"Thirty seconds!" Burgess screamed tensely.

Mr. Crepsley ignored the interruption. "If we are captured and taken alive, there may be chances to escape later. But if we kill Steve Leonard, I do not think they will spare us. These humans are ready to butcher us at the drop of a pin."

Vancha shook his head uncertainly. "I don't like it. I'd rather kill him and take our chances."

"I would too," Mr. Crepsley agreed. "But there is the Vampaneze Lord to consider. We must put the hunt before our personal wishes. Sparing Steve Leonard is —"

"Ten seconds!" Burgess bellowed.

Vancha glowered over Steve a few seconds more, undecided, then cursed, twisted his hand, and whacked him over the back of the head with the flat of his palm. Steve toppled to the floor. I thought Vancha had killed him, but the Prince had only knocked him out.

"That should shut him up for a while," Vancha grunted, checking his shuriken belts and wrapping his animal hides tight around him. "If we get the chance later, we'll track him down and finish him off."

"Time's up!" Alice Burgess warned us. "Come out immediately or we open fire!"

"Ready?" Vancha asked.

"Ready," Mr. Crepsley said, drawing his knives.

"Ready," Harkat said, testing the head of his axe with a large, grey finger.

"Ready," I said, taking out my sword and holding it across my chest.

"Harkat jumps with me," Vancha said. "Larten and Darren — you come next. Give us a second or two to roll out of your way."

"Luck, Vancha," Mr. Crepsley said.

"Luck," Vancha replied, then grinned savagely, slapped Harkat on the back, and leaped through the window, shattering the blind and glass, Harkat not far behind.

Mr. Crepsley and I waited the agreed seconds, then jumped through the jagged remains of the window after our friends, and dropped swiftly to the ground like a couple of wingless bats, into the hellish cauldron that awaited us below.

CHAPTER FOUR

As THE GROUND rushed up to meet me, I brought my legs together, hunched my upper body, spread my hands, and landed in a crouch. My extra-strong bones absorbed the shock without breaking, although the force of the contact sent me rolling forward and I almost impaled myself on my sword (which would have been an embarrassing way to die).

There was a sharp yell of pain to my left, and as I bounced onto my feet I saw Mr. Crepsley lying on the ground, nursing his right ankle, unable to stand. Ignoring my injured friend, I brought up my sword defensively and looked for Vancha and Harkat.

Our leap through the window had taken the police and soldiers by surprise. They were falling over one another and getting in each other's way, making it impossible for anyone to take a clean shot.

Harkat had grabbed a young soldier in the midst of the confusion and was holding him close to his chest, spinning quickly in circles so nobody had time to shoot him in the back. Vancha, meanwhile, had set his sights on the big cheese. As I watched, he charged through several officers and soldiers, leaped over a car, and brought Chief Inspector Alice Burgess crashing to the ground with a perfectly timed tackle.

While all human eyes fixed on Vancha and the Chief Inspector, I hurried to Mr. Crepsley's side and helped him up. His teeth were gritted in pain and I could tell instantly that his ankle wouldn't support him.

"Is it broken?" I shouted, dragging him behind a car for cover before someone snapped to his senses and took a shot at us.

"I do not think so," he gasped, "but the pain is intense." He collapsed behind the car and rubbed the flesh around his ankle, trying to massage out the pain.

Across the way, Vancha was on his feet, Alice Burgess's throat clutched in one hand, her megaphone in the other. "Hear this!" he roared through the megaphone at the police and soldiers. "If you shoot, your Chief dies!"

Above us, the blades of the helicopter hummed like the wings of a thousand angry bees. Otherwise — total silence.

Burgess broke it. "Forget about me!" she roared. "Take these creeps out now!"

Several marksmen raised their weapons obediently.

Vancha tightened his fingers around the police chief's throat. Her eyes bulged worryingly. The marksmen hesitated, then lowered their weapons slightly. Vancha loosened his grip, but didn't let go completely. Holding the white-haired woman in front of him, he shuffled over to where Harkat was standing with his human shield. The two got back to back, then slowly crossed to where Mr. Crepsley and I were sheltering. They resembled a large and clumsy crab as they moved, but it worked. Nobody fired.

"How bad is it?" Vancha asked, crouching beside us, dragging Burgess down with him. Harkat did likewise with his soldier.

"Bad," Mr. Crepsley said soberly, locking gazes with Vancha.

"You can't flit?" Vancha asked softly.

"Not like this."

They stared at each other silently.

"Then we'll have to leave you behind," Vancha said.

"Aye." Mr. Crepsley smiled thinly.

"I'm staying with him," I said instantly.

"This is no time for false heroics," Vancha growled. "You're coming — end of story."

I shook my head. "The hell with false heroics — I'm being practical. You can't flit with both me and Harkat on your back. It would take too long to work up the speed. We'd be shot dead before we got to the end of the street."

Vancha opened his mouth to object, realized my argument was valid, and closed it.

"I'm staying too," Harkat said.

Vancha groaned. "We don't have time for this rubbish!"

"It's not rubbish," Harkat said calmly. "I travel with Darren. Where he goes, I go. Where he stays, I stay. Besides, you'll stand a better chance . . . without me."

"How do you figure that?" Vancha asked.

Harkat pointed at Alice Burgess, still gasping from the tightness of Vancha's grip. "Alone, you can carry her and use her as a . . . shield until you flit."

Vancha sighed downheartedly. "You're all too clever for me. I'm not going to sit here and try to talk you round." He stuck his head up over the bonnet of the car to check on the surrounding troops, squinting hard against the daylight. "Stay back," he warned, "or these two die!"

"You'll . . . never get . . . away," Burgess croaked, her pale blue eyes filled with hate, her ghostly white skin flushed a deep, angry red. "The first . . . clear shot they have . . . they'll take you out!"

"Then we'll have to make sure we don't give them one," Vancha laughed, covering her mouth with a hand before she could reply. His smile faded. "I can't come back for you," he said to us. "If you stay, you're on your own."

"We know," Mr. Crepsley said.

Vancha glanced up at the sun. "You'd better surrender straightaway and pray to the gods that they bundle you into a cell without windows."

"Aye." Mr. Crepsley's teeth were chattering, partly from the pain in his ankle, partly from fear of the deadly rays of the sun.

Leaning forward, Vancha whispered so that Burgess and the soldier couldn't hear. "If I escape, I'll return for the Vampaneze Lord. I'll wait in the cavern where we fought last night. I'll give you until midnight. If you aren't there by then, I'll go after him alone."

Mr. Crepsley nodded. "We will do our best to break out. If I cannot walk, Darren and Harkat will escape without me." He stared searchingly at us. "*Yes?*"

"Yes," Harkat said.

I stared back silently a moment longer, then dropped my gaze. "Yes," I muttered reluctantly.

Vancha grunted, then stuck out his free hand. We all joined a hand to his. "Luck," he said, and each of us repeated it in turn.

Then, without waiting, Vancha stood and walked away, Burgess held stiffly in front of him. He'd dropped the megaphone on his way over. Now he stopped to pick it up and address the troops again. "I'm making a break for it!" he bellowed pleasantly. "I know it's your job to stop me, but if you fire, your boss dies too. If you're wise, you'll wait for me to make an error. After all," he chuckled, "you've got cars and helicopters. I'm on foot. I'm sure you can keep pace with me until the time's right to pounce."

Tossing aside the megaphone, Vancha lifted the Chief Inspector off the ground, held her in front of him like a doll, and ran.

A senior officer darted for the megaphone, snatched it up, and issued orders. "Hold your fire!" he shouted. "Don't break ranks. Wait for him to tumble or drop her. He can't escape. Train your sights on him, wait for a clean shot, then let him have it in the —"

He stopped abruptly. He'd been watching Vancha race toward a blockade at the end of the street as he was talking, but in the blink of an eye the vampire had disappeared. Vancha had hit flitting speed, and to the humans it seemed as if he'd simply vanished into thin air.

As the police and soldiers crowded forward in disbelief, guns cocked, staring at the ground as though they thought Vancha and their Chief had sunk into it, Mr. Crepsley, Harkat, and I grinned at each other.

"At least one of us is in the clear," Mr. Crepsley said.

"We would have been too, if you weren't such a clumsy ox," I grunted.

Mr. Crepsley glanced up at the sun and his smile slipped. "If they leave me in a cell which is open to the sun," he said quietly, "I will not wait to burn to death. I will escape or die trying."

I nodded grimly. "We all will."

Harkat pulled his soldier around so that he was facing us. The young man's face was green with terror and he was incapable of speech.

"Do we leave him or . . . try to use him as a bargaining chip?" Harkat asked.

"Leave him," I said. "They're less likely to shoot if we give ourselves up freely. If we try bargaining now, after Vancha has escaped with their boss, I think they'll mow us down."

"We must leave our weapons too," Mr. Crepsley said, laying his knives aside.

I didn't want to part with my sword, but common sense prevailed and I left it in a heap with Mr.

Crepsley's knives, Harkat's axe, and the other bits and pieces we'd been carrying. Then we rolled up the arms of our sleeves, raised our hands above our heads, shouted that we were surrendering, and walked out — Mr. Crepsley hopping on one leg — to be arrested and imprisoned by the dark-faced, trigger-itchy officers of the law, who handcuffed us, cursed us, bundled us into vans, and drove us away — to prison.

CHAPTER FIVE

I WAS IN A CELL no more than thirteen feet by thirteen, with a ceiling maybe ten feet high. There were no windows — apart from a small one set in the door — and no two-way mirrors. There were two surveillance cameras in the corners above the door, a long table with a tape recorder on it, three chairs, me — and three grim-looking police officers.

One of the officers was standing by the door, a rifle cradled tightly across his chest, eyes sharp. He hadn't told me his name — he hadn't spoken a word — but I could read it from his badge: William McKay.

The other two weren't wearing badges, but had told me their names: Con and Ivan. Con was tall, dark-faced, and very lean, with a gruff manner and ready sneer. Ivan was older and thinner, with grey hair.

He looked tired and spoke softly, as though the questions were exhausting him.

"Is Darren Shan your real name, like we've been told?" Ivan inquired for about the twentieth time since I'd been admitted to the holding cell. They'd been asking the same questions over and over, and showed no signs of letting up.

I didn't answer. So far I hadn't said anything.

"Or is it Darren Horston — the name you've been using recently?" Ivan asked after a few seconds of silence.

No answer.

"How about your traveling companion — Larten Crepsley or Vur Horston?"

I looked down at my hands, which were handcuffed, and said nothing. I examined the chain linking the handcuffs: steel, short, thick. I thought I'd be able to snap it if I had to, but I wasn't sure.

My ankles were cuffed as well. The chain linking my ankles had been short when I was arrested. The police left the short chain on while I was being fingerprinted and photographed, but took it off and replaced it with a longer chain soon after they locked me away securely in the cell.

"What about the freak?" the officer called Con asked. "That grey-skinned monster. What's —"

"He isn't a monster!" I snapped, breaking my code of silence.

"Oh?" Con sneered. "What is he then?"

I shook my head. "You wouldn't believe me if I told you."

"Try us," Ivan encouraged me, but I only shook my head again.

"What about the other two?" Con asked. "Vancha March and Larten Crepsley. Our informants told us they were vampires. What do you have to say about that?"

I smiled humorlessly. "Vampires don't exist," I said. "Everyone knows that."

"That's right," Ivan said. "They don't." He leaned across the table, as though to tell me a secret. "But those two aren't entirely normal, Darren, as I'm sure you already know. March disappeared like a magician, while Crepsley . . ." He coughed. "Well, we haven't been able to photograph him."

I smiled when he said that, and looked up at the video cameras. Full-vampires have peculiar atoms, which make it impossible for them to be captured on film. The police could take snaps of Mr. Crepsley from every angle they could dream of, with the best cameras available — to no visible effect.

"Look at the grin on him!" Con snapped. "He thinks this is funny!"

"No," I said, wiping the smile from my face. "I don't."

"Then why are you laughing?"

I shrugged. "I was thinking of something else."

Ivan slumped back in his chair, disappointed by my answers. "We've taken a blood sample from Crepsley," he said. "From the thing called Harkat Mulds too. We'll find out what they are when the results come back. It would be to your advantage to tell us now."

I didn't reply. Ivan waited a moment, then ran a hand through his grey hair. He sighed despondently, and began with the questions again. "What's your real name? What's your relationship to the others? Where . . ."

More time passed. I wasn't able to judge exactly how long I'd been imprisoned. It felt like a day or more, but realistically it was probably only four or five hours, maybe less. The sun was most likely still shining outside.

I thought about Mr. Crepsley and wondered how he was faring. If he was in a cell like mine, he'd nothing to worry about. But if they'd put him in a cell with windows . . .

"Where are my friends?" I asked.

Con and Ivan had been discussing something under their breath. Now they looked at me, expressions guarded.

"You'd like to see them?" Ivan asked.

"I just want to know where they are," I said.

"If you answer our questions, a meeting can be arranged," Ivan promised.

"I just want to know where they are," I repeated.

"They're close," Con grunted. "Locked away nice and tight like you."

"In cells like this?" I asked.

"Exactly the same," Con said, then looked around at the walls and smiled as he realized why I was concerned. "Cells without windows," he chuckled, then nudged his partner in the ribs. "But that can be changed, can't it, Ivan? What say we move the 'vampire' to a cell with lovely round windows? A cell with a view of the outside . . . the sky . . . the *sun*."

I said nothing, but locked gazes with Con and stared back angrily.

"You don't like the sound of that, do you?" Con hissed. "The thought of us sticking Crepsley in a room with windows terrifies you, doesn't it?"

I shrugged indifferently and averted my eyes. "I want to speak to a lawyer," I said.

Con burst out laughing. Ivan hid a smile behind a

hand. Even the guard with the rifle smirked, as though I'd cracked the best joke ever.

"What's so funny?" I snapped. "I know my rights. I'm entitled to a phone call and a lawyer."

"Of course," Con crowed. "Even killers have rights." He rapped the table with his knuckles, then turned off the tape recorder. "But guess what — we're withholding those rights. We'll catch hell for it later, but we don't care. We've got you walled up here and we won't let you take advantage of your rights until you give us some answers."

"That's illegal," I growled. "You can't do that."

"Normally, no," he agreed. "Normally our Chief Inspector would barge in and kick up a storm if she heard about something like this. But our Chief isn't here, is she? She's been abducted by your fellow killer, Vancha March."

I went white-lipped when I heard that and realized what it meant. With their Chief out of the way, they'd taken the law into their own hands, and were prepared to do whatever it took to find out where she was and get her back. It might cost them their careers, but they didn't care. This was personal.

"You'll have to torture me to make me talk," I said stiffly, testing them to see how far they were willing to go.

"Torture's not our way," Ivan said immediately. "We don't do things like that."

"Unlike some people we could mention," Con added, then tossed a photo across the table at me. I tried to ignore it, but my eyes flicked automatically to the figure in it. I saw that it was the vampet we'd taken hostage earlier that morning in the tunnels, the one called Mark Ryter — the one Vancha had tortured and killed.

"We're not evil," I said quietly. But I could see things from their point of view and understood how monstrous we must look. "There are sides to this you don't know about. We're not the killers you seek. We're trying to stop them, the same as you."

Con barked a laugh.

"It's true," I insisted. "Mark Ryter was one of the bad guys. We had to hurt him to find out about the others. We're not your enemies. You and I are on the same side."

"That's the weakest lie I've ever heard," Con snapped. "How dumb do you think we are?"

"I don't think you're dumb at all," I said. "But you're misguided. You've been tricked. You . . ." I leaned forward eagerly. "Who told you where to find us? Who told you our names, that we were vampires, that we were your killers?"

The policemen shared an uneasy glance, then Ivan said, "It was an anonymous tip-off. The caller rang from a public phone booth, left no name, and was gone when we arrived."

"Doesn't that sound fishy to you?" I asked.

"We receive anonymous tips all the time," Ivan said, but he looked fidgety and I knew he had his doubts. If he'd been alone, maybe I could have talked him round to my way of thinking, and persuaded him to grant me the benefit of the doubt. But before I could say anything more, Con tossed another photo across the table at me, then another. Close-ups of Mark Ryter, capturing even more of the grisly details than the first.

"People on *our* side don't kill other people," he said coldly. "Even when they'd like to," he added meaningfully, pointing a finger at me.

I sighed and let it drop, knowing I couldn't convince them of my innocence. A few seconds of silence passed, while they settled down after the exchange and composed themselves. Then they switched the tape recorder on and the questions started again. Who was I? Where had I come from? Where did Vancha March go? How many people had we killed? On and on and on and . . .

The police were getting nowhere with me, and it was frustrating them. Ivan and Con had been joined by another officer called Morgan, who had pinpoint eyes and dark brown hair. He sat stiff-backed, his hands flat on the table, subjecting me to a cool, unbreaking gaze. I had the feeling that Morgan was here to get nasty, although so far he'd made no violent moves against me.

"How old are you?" Con was asking. "Where are you from? How long have you been here? Why pick this city? How many others have you murdered? Where are the bodies? What have —"

He stopped at a knock on the door. Turning away, he went to see who was there. Ivan's eyes followed Con as he went, but Morgan's stayed on me. He blinked once every four seconds, no more, no less, like a robot.

Con had a murmured conversation with the person outside the door, then stood back and motioned the guard with the rifle away. The guard sidestepped over to the wall and trained his weapon on me, making sure I wouldn't try anything funny.

I was expecting another police officer, or maybe a soldier — I hadn't seen anyone from the army since I'd been arrested — but the meek little man who entered took me by complete surprise.

"*Mr. Blaws?*" I gasped.

The school inspector who'd forced me to go to Mahler's looked nervous. He was carrying the same huge briefcase as before, and wearing the same old-fashioned bowler hat. He advanced half a yard, then stopped, reluctant to come any closer.

"Thank you for coming, Walter," Ivan said, rising to shake the visitor's hand.

Mr. Blaws nodded feebly and squeaked, "Glad to be of assistance."

"Would you like a chair?" Ivan asked.

Mr. Blaws shook his head quickly. "No, thanks. I'd rather not stop any longer than necessary. Rounds to do. Places to be. You know how it is."

Ivan nodded sympathetically. "That's fine. You brought the papers?"

Mr. Blaws nodded. "The forms he filled in, all the files we have on him. Yes. I left them with a man at the front desk. He's photocopying them and giving the originals back to me before I leave. I have to hold on to the originals for the school records."

"Fine," Ivan said again, then stepped aside and jerked his head at me. "Can you identify this boy?" he asked officiously.

"Yes," Mr. Blaws said. "He's Darren Horston. He enrolled with Mahler's on the . . ." He paused and frowned. "I've forgotten the exact date. I should know it, because I was looking at it on the way in."

"That's OK." Ivan smiled. "We'll get it from the photocopies. But this is definitely the boy who called himself Darren Horston? You're sure?"

Mr. Blaws nodded firmly. "Oh yes," he said. "I never forget the face of a pupil, especially one who's played truant."

"Thank you, Walter," Ivan said, taking the school inspector's arm. "If we need you again, we'll . . ."

He stopped. Mr. Blaws hadn't moved. He was staring at me with wide eyes and a trembling lip. "Is it true?" Mr. Blaws asked. "What the media are saying — he and his friends are the killers?"

Ivan hesitated. "We can't really say right now, but as soon as we —"

"How could you?" Mr. Blaws shouted at me. "How could you kill all those people? And poor little Tara Williams — your own classmate!"

"I didn't kill Tara," I said tiredly. "I didn't kill anybody. I'm not a killer. The police have arrested the wrong people."

"Hah!" Con snorted.

"You're a beast," Mr. Blaws growled, raising his briefcase high in the air, as though he meant to throw it at me. "You should be . . . you should . . . should . . ."

He couldn't say any more. His lips tightened and his jaw clenched shut. Turning his back on me, he started out of the door. As he was stepping through, I reacted to a childish impulse and called him back.

"Mr. Blaws?" I shouted. He paused and looked over his shoulder questioningly. I adopted an innocent, dismayed expression. "This won't harm my grades, will it, sir?" I inquired sweetly.

The school inspector gaped at me, then glared furiously when he realized I was teasing him, turned up his nose, showed me a clean pair of heels and clacked away down the corridor.

I laughed aloud as Mr. Blaws departed, taking absurd comfort in the annoying little man's irate expression. Con, Ivan, and the guard with the gun smiled too, despite themselves, but Morgan didn't. He remained as steely-faced as ever, a terrible, unspoken menace in his sharp, mechanical eyes.

CHAPTER SIX

IVAN WAS REPLACED by a burly police officer called Dave shortly after Mr. Blaws had departed. Dave acted friendly — the first thing he did when he came in was ask me if I'd like anything to eat or drink — but I wasn't fooled. I'd watched enough TV shows to know all about the good cop/bad cop routine.

"We're here to help you, Darren," Dave assured me, tearing open a packet of sugar and pouring it into a plastic cup filled with steaming coffee. Some of the sugar spilled over the side, onto the table. I was ninety percent certain the spill was deliberate — Dave wanted me to think he was a bumbler.

"Taking off these handcuffs and setting me free would be a big help," I quipped, watching Dave cautiously as he tore open another packet of sugar. Morgan worried me the most — Con might knock me around a bit, if things got rough, but I believed Morgan was capable of worse — but I'd have to be extra careful with Dave, or he'd worm my secrets out of me. I'd been awake a long time. I was drained and light-headed. Prone to slips.

"Take off your handcuffs and set you free," Dave smirked, winking at me. "Good one. Of course, we both know that isn't going to happen, but there are things I *can* do. Get you a lawyer for one. A bath. A change of clothes. A nice bunk for the night. You're going to be with us a long time, I fear, but it doesn't have to be an unpleasant stay."

"What do I have to do to make it *pleasant*?" I asked cagily.

Dave shrugged and sipped the coffee. "Ouch! Too hot!" Fanning his lips with a hand to cool them down, he smiled. "Not much," he said in answer to my question. "Tell us your real name, where you're from, what you're doing here. That kind of stuff."

I shook my head wryly — new face, same old questions.

Dave saw I wasn't going to answer, so he changed tack. "That routine's stale, right? Let's try something else. Your friend, Harkat Mulds, says he needs his mask to survive, that he'll die if exposed to air for more than ten or twelve hours. Is that true?"

I nodded cautiously. "Yes."

Dave looked glum. "This is bad," he muttered. "Very, very bad."

"What do you mean?" I asked.

"This is a prison, Darren. You and your friends are murder suspects. There are rules . . . guidelines . . . things we must do. Taking objects like belts, ties, and *masks* from possible killers when they're admitted is one of the rules."

I stiffened in my chair. "You've taken away Harkat's mask?" I snapped.

"We had to," Dave said.

"But he'll die without it!"

Dave rolled his shoulders carelessly. "We have only your word for that. It's not enough. But if you tell us what he is and why normal air is deadly for him . . . and if you tell us about your other friends, Crepsley and March . . . maybe we can help."

I glared hatefully at the policeman. "So it's rat on my friends or you'll let Harkat die?" I sneered.

"That's a horrible way to put it," Dave protested warmly. "We don't intend to let any of you die. If your short, unusual friend takes a turn for the worse, we'll hurry him down to the medical wing and patch him up, like we're doing for the man you took hostage. But —"

"Steve's here?" I interrupted. "You've got Steve Leopard in the medical wing?"

"Steve *Leonard*," he corrected me, unaware of Steve's nickname. "We brought him here to recover. Easier to guard him from the media."

That was great news. I thought we'd lost Steve. If we could get to him when we were escaping and take him with us, we could use him when it came to trying to save Debbie's life.

I stretched my chained hands above my head and yawned. "What's the time?" I asked casually.

"Sorry," Dave smiled. "That's classified information."

I lowered my arms. "You know you asked me earlier if there was anything I wanted?"

"Uh-huh," Dave replied, eyes narrowing hopefully.

"Would it be OK if I walked around for a few minutes? My legs are cramping up."

Dave looked disappointed — he'd been anticipating a more involved request. "You can't leave this room," he said.

"I'm not asking to. A couple of minutes pacing from one side to the other will be fine."

Dave checked with Con and Morgan to see what they thought.

"Let him," Con said, "as long as he stays on his own side of the table."

Morgan didn't say anything, just nodded once to show it was OK.

Pushing my chair back, I stood, stepped away from the table, jangled the chain linking my ankles together, loosening it, then walked from one wall to the other, stretching my legs, working the tension out of my muscles, formulating an escape plan.

After a while I stopped at one of the walls and rested my forehead against it. I began lightly kicking the lower part of the wall with my left foot, as if I was nervous and claustrophobic. In reality I was testing it. I wanted to know how thick the wall was and if I could break through.

The results of the test were unpromising. By the feel of the wall, and the dull echoes from my kicks, it was made of solid concrete, two or three blocks thick. I could bust through eventually, but it would take a lot of work and — more crucially — time. The guard by the door would have ample opportunity to raise his weapon and fire.

Levering myself away from the wall, I started walking again, eyes flicking from the door to the wall at the front of the cell. The door looked pretty solid —

steel — but maybe the wall it was set in wasn't as thick as the others. Perhaps I could break through it quicker than through the sides or back. Wait until it was definitely night, hope the police let me alone in the cell, then smash through and . . .

No. Even if the police left me, the video cameras set in the corners above the door wouldn't. Someone would be watching all the time. The alarm would sound as soon as I attacked the wall, and the corridor outside would fill with police within seconds.

It had to be the ceiling. From where I stood, I had no idea whether it was reinforced or normal, if I could punch a way through or not. But it was the only logical escape route. If I was left alone, I could knock out the cameras, take to the rafters, and hopefully lose my pursuers along the way. I wouldn't have time to search for Harkat and Mr. Crepsley, so I'd just have to hope they made it out by themselves.

It wasn't much of a plan — I still hadn't figured out how I was going to get the policemen to leave; I didn't think they'd withdraw for the night to let me catch up on my beauty sleep — but at least it was the beginning of one. The rest would fall into place along the way.

I hoped!

I walked for a few minutes more, then Dave asked

me to sit again, and we were back to the questions. This time they came quicker than before, more urgently. I got the sense that their patience was nearing its end. Violence couldn't be far off.

The police were increasing the pressure. The offers of food and drinks were no longer being made, and Dave's smile was a slim shadow of its former self. The large officer had loosened his collar button and was sweating freely as he pounded me with question after question. He'd given up asking about my name and background. Now he wanted to know how many people I'd killed, where the bodies were, and if I was just an accomplice or an active member of the murderous gang.

In reply to his questions I kept saying, "I didn't kill anyone. I'm not your enemy. You have the wrong person."

Con wasn't as polite as Dave. He'd started slamming the table with his fists and leaning forward menacingly every time he addressed me. I believed he was only minutes away from setting about me with his fists, and steeled myself against the blows that seemed sure to come.

Morgan hadn't changed. He sat quiet and still, staring relentlessly, blinking once every four seconds.

"Are there others?" Dave growled. "Is it just the four of you, or are there more killers in the gang that we don't know about?"

"We're not killers," I sighed, rubbing my eyes, trying to stay alert.

"Did you kill them first, then drink from them, or was it the other way around?" Dave pressed.

I shook my head and didn't reply.

"Do you really believe you're vampires, or is that a cover story, or some sick game you like to indulge in?"

"Leave me alone," I whispered, dropping my gaze. "You've got it all wrong. We're not your enemies."

"How many have you killed?" Dave roared. "Where are —"

He stopped. People had poured into the corridor outside during the last few seconds, and now it was teeming with police and staff, all shouting wildly.

"What the hell's going on?" Dave snapped.

"Want me to check?" William McKay — the guard with the rifle — asked.

"No," Con responded. "I'll do it. You keep a watch on the boy."

Going to the door, Con banged on it and called for it to be opened. There was no immediate response, so he called again, louder, and this time it swung open. Stepping out, the dark-faced officer grabbed a woman who was rushing past and quickly shook a few answers out of her.

Con had to lean in close to the woman to hear what she was saying. When he had it straight, he let go of her and rushed back into my cell, eyes wide. "It's a breakout!" Con shouted.

"Which one?" Dave yelled, jumping up. "Crepsley? Mulds?"

"Neither," Con gasped. "It's the hostage — Steve Leonard!"

"*Leonard?*" Dave repeated uncertainly. "But he's not a prisoner. Why should he want to break —"

"I don't know!" Con shouted. "Apparently, he regained consciousness a few minutes ago, took stock of the situation, then murdered a guard and two nurses."

The color drained from Dave's face, and William McKay almost dropped his rifle.

"A guard and two . . ." Dave murmured.

"That's not all," Con said. "He's killed or wounded another three on his way out. They think he's still in the building."

Dave's face hardened. He started for the door, then remembered me, paused, and looked back over his shoulder.

"I'm not a killer," I said quietly, staring him straight in the eye. "I'm not the one you want. I'm on your side."

This time, I think he half-believed me.

"What about me?" William McKay asked as the two officers filed out. "Do I stay or go?"

"Come with us," Con snapped.

"What about the boy?"

"I'll take care of him," Morgan said softly. His eyes hadn't strayed from my face, even while Con was telling Dave about Steve. The guard hurried out after the others, slamming the door shut behind him.

I was alone at last — with Morgan.

The officer with the tiny, watchful eyes sat staring at me. Four seconds — blink. Eight seconds — blink. Twelve seconds — blink.

He leaned forward, turned off the tape recorder, then stood and stretched. "I thought we'd never get rid of them," he said. Strolling to the door, he glanced out of the small window set high in it, and spoke softly, his face hidden from the cameras overhead. "You'll have to go through the ceiling, but you had figured that out already, hadn't you?"

"Excuse me?" I said, startled.

"I saw you casing the room while you were 'exercising,'" he smiled. "The walls are too thick. You don't have time to break through."

I said nothing, but stared hard at the brown-haired officer, wondering what he was up to.

"I'm going to attack you in a minute," Morgan said. "I'll put on a show for the cameras, pretend to lose my temper and go for your throat. Slam me over the head with your fists, hard, and I'll go down for the count. After that it's up to you. I have no key for your chains, so you'll have to snap out of them yourself. If you can't — tough. Nor can I guarantee how much time you'll have, but with all the panic in the halls outside, there should be plenty."

"Why are you doing this?" I asked, stunned by the unexpected turn of events.

"You'll see," Morgan said, spinning to face me, then advancing in what would appear on camera to be a violent, threatening manner. "I'll be helpless when I hit the floor," Morgan said, waving his arms about wildly. "If you decide to kill me, I won't be able to stop you. But from what I've heard, you're not the sort to kill a defenseless opponent."

"Why should I want to kill you when you're helping me escape?" I asked, bewildered.

Morgan grinned nastily. "You'll see," he said again, then dived over the table at me.

I was so amazed by what was happening, that when he wrapped his hands around my throat, I didn't do anything, just stared back at him uncertainly. Then he squeezed tightly and self-preservation kicked in. Jerking my head backward, I brought up my chained hands and shoved him away. He slapped at my hands, then came at me again. Lurching to my feet, I pushed his head down, held it between my knees, raised my arms, brought my hands together, and smashed him over the back of his head.

With a grunt, Morgan slid off the table, dropped to the floor and lay there motionless. I was worried that I'd really hurt him. Hurrying around the table, I bent to check his pulse. As I leaned down, I got close enough to his head to see through his thin layer of hair to the scalp beneath. What I saw sent a flash chill racing down my spine. Underneath the hair, tattooed into the flesh, was a large, rough "V" — the mark of the vampets!

"Yuh-yuh-yuh-you're . . . ," I stuttered.

"Yes," Morgan said softly. He'd landed with his left arm thrown over his face, hiding his mouth and eyes from the lens of the camera. "And proud to serve the rightful rulers of the night."

I reeled away from the police vampet, more unnerved than ever. I'd thought the vampets served alongside their masters. It never occurred to me that some could be working undercover as ordinary humans.

Morgan opened his left eye and glanced up at me without moving. "You'd better get moving," he hissed, "before the cavalry arrives."

Remembering where I was and what was at stake, I got to my feet and tried not to dwell on the shock of finding a vampet here among the police. I wanted to leap onto the table and make my escape via the ceiling, but first there were the cameras to take care of. Bending, I picked up the tape recorder, quickly crossed the room and used the base of the recorder to shatter the video cameras, rendering them useless.

"Very good," Morgan whispered as I retraced my steps. "Very clever. Now fly, little bat. Fly like the devil is after you."

Pausing over the vampet, I glared down at him, drew back my right foot as far as my chains would allow, and kicked him hard in the side of the head. He grunted, rolled over and lay still. I didn't know if he was really unconscious or if this was part of his act, and I didn't stay to find out.

Jumping onto the table, I stuck my hands together, paused, then wrenched my wrists apart as sharply as possible, using all of my vampiric powers. I almost dislocated my lower arms, and roared aloud with pain, but it worked — the chain joining my handcuffs snapped in the middle, freeing my hands.

I stood on the ends of the chain linking my ankles, grabbed it in the middle and pulled upwards quickly. *Too* quickly — I rolled back off the table and collapsed in a heap on the floor!

Groaning, I rolled over, got up, stood on the chain again, braced my back against a wall, and made a second stab at the chain. This time I was successful and it snapped in two. I wrapped the twin lengths of chain around my ankles, to prevent them snagging on corners, then did the same thing with the chains dangling from my wrists.

I was ready. Hopping onto the table again, I crouched, took a deep breath, then leaped, the fingers of both hands held out flat and straight.

The ceiling, thankfully, was made of ordinary plaster tiles, and my fingers burst through with only the barest of resistance. Sweeping my hands apart while hovering in midair, my forearms connected with rafters on either side. Splaying my fingers, I caught hold of the lengths of wood as gravity dragged me back to earth, and held firm, halting my fall.

I hung there a moment, until I stopped swinging, then hauled my legs and body out of the cell, up into darkness and the freedom it promised.

CHAPTER SEVEN

THERE WAS A GAP of one and a half feet between the rafters I was lying on and those overhead. It wasn't much, and it made life very uncomfortable, but it was more than I'd expected.

Stretching out flat, I listened for sounds of pursuit in the cell below. There weren't any. I could hear people colliding with each other and barking out orders in the corridor, so either the police weren't aware I'd broken out, or had found their way blocked by the panicked crowds.

Whatever the answer, I had time on my side; time I hadn't bargained for, which I could put to good use. I'd planned to flee as swiftly as possible, leaving Mr. Crepsley and Harkat behind, but now I was in a position to go and look for them.

But where to look? The light was pretty good up

here — there were many cracks between the plaster tiles, and light seeped up from the rooms and corridors below — and I could see for ten or twelve yards whichever way I looked. This was a big building, and if my friends were being held on another floor, I didn't have a hope in hell of finding them. But if they were nearby, and I hurried . . .

Scuttling over the rafters, I reached the ceiling of the cell next to mine, paused, and cocked my ears. My sharp sense of hearing would detect any sound above that of a heartbeat. I waited a few seconds, but heard nothing. I moved on.

The next two cells were empty. In the third I heard someone scratching himself. I thought about calling out Mr. Crepsley's and Harkat's names, but if there were police in the cell, they would raise the alarm. There was only one thing to do. Taking a deep breath, I gripped the rafters on either side with my hands and feet, then punched through the thin material of the ceiling with my head.

I blew dust from my lips and blinked it out of my eyes, then focused on the scene below. I was ready to drop through the ceiling if either of my friends was within, but the only occupant was a bearded old man who stared up at me, mouth agape, blinking rapidly.

"Sorry," I said, forcing a quick smile. "Wrong room."

Withdrawing, I scurried forward, leaving the startled prisoner behind.

Three more empty cells. The next was occupied, but by two loud-talking men who'd been captured trying to rob a corner shop. I didn't stop to check on them — the police were hardly likely to lump a potential killer in with a couple of burglars.

Another empty cell. I thought the next was empty too, and had almost moved on when my ears picked up on the faint rustling of fabric. I came to a halt and listened intently, but there were no further sounds. Crawling backward, skin itching from the insulting flakes that littered the ceiling tiles like snow, I got into position, took another deep breath, then head-butted through the tiles.

A wary Harkat Mulds jumped out of the chair he'd been sitting in and brought his arms up defensively as my head broke through and clouds of dust descended. Then the Little Person saw who it was, reached up, tore loose his mask (Dave had obviously been lying when he said they'd taken it away) and shouted my name with unconstrained delight. "*Darren*!"

"Howdy, pardner." I grinned, using my hands to

widen the hole. I shook the dust from my hair and eyebrows.

"What are you doing . . . up there?" Harkat asked.

I groaned at the dumb question. "Sightseeing!" I snapped, then lowered a hand. "C'mon — we don't have much time, and we have to find Mr. Crepsley."

I'm sure Harkat had a thousand questions — I had too, like how come he was all alone, and why wasn't he handcuffed? — but he realized how perilous our position was, grabbed the offered hand, and let me drag him up, saying nothing.

He had a harder time squeezing onto the rafters than me — his body was a lot rounder than mine — but finally he was lying out flat beside me and we crawled forward, side by side, without discussing our plight.

The next eight or nine cells were empty or occupied by humans. I was growing anxious about the amount of time that had passed. Regardless of what was happening with Steve Leopard, my escape was bound to be noticed sooner rather than later, and pursuit would be fierce when it came. I was wondering whether it would be wiser to quit while we were ahead, when someone spoke from a spot in the cell underneath, just ahead of me.

"I am ready to make a statement now," said the

voice, and by the second syllable I had the speaker pegged — Mr. Crepsley!

I held up a hand for Harkat to stop, but he'd heard it too and had already come to a standstill (or rather, a *crawl*still).

"About time," a policeman said. "Let me check that our recorder's working . . ."

"Never mind your infernal recording device," Mr. Crepsley sniffed. "I do not address myself to inanimate machines. Nor do I waste words on buffoons. I will speak to neither you nor your partner on my left. As for that cretin by the door with the rifle . . ."

I had to stifle a giggle. The sly old fox! He must have heard us crawling about up here and was letting us know exactly how things stood in the cell, how many police were present, and where they were.

"You'd better watch yourself," the policeman snapped. "I've a good mind to —"

"You have no sort of mind at all," Mr. Crepsley interrupted. "You are a fool. The officer who was here earlier, on the other hand — Matt — struck me as a sensible man. Fetch him and I will confess. Otherwise my lips remain sealed."

The officer cursed, then shuffled to his feet and started for the door. "Keep an eye on him," he told the other two. "The first sign of a twitch — hit him hard! Remember who and what he is. Take no chances."

"Find out what the fuss is about while you're out there," one of the other officers said as his colleague was leaving. "The way people are rushing about, there must be some emergency."

"Will do," the officer said, then called for the door to be opened and let himself out.

I pointed Harkat off to the left, where the guard by the door would be. He slid forward silently, stopping when he got a fix on the policeman. I listened for sounds of the officer closer to Mr. Crepsley, tuned into his heavy breathing, shifted back a yard or so, then held my left hand up, the thumb and first two fingers spread. I counted to two and lowered my middle finger. Another couple of seconds and I bent down my index finger. Finally, nodding swiftly at Harkat, I lowered my thumb.

At the signal, Harkat let go of the rafters and dropped through the plaster tiles of the ceiling, smashing them to pieces in the process. I followed almost instantly, bringing my legs down first, howling like a wolf for added effect.

The policemen didn't know what to make of our sudden appearance. The guard by the door tried to bring his rifle up, but Harkat's plummeting body collided with his arms and knocked it free of his grip. My officer, meanwhile, only gaped at me, making no move to protect himself.

While Harkat clambered to his feet and threw punches at the guard, I drew a fist back to let the officer have a bunch of fives in the face. Mr. Crepsley stopped me. "Please," he said politely, getting to his feet and tapping the officer on the shoulder. "Let me."

The officer turned as though hypnotized. Mr. Crepsley opened his mouth and breathed the special knockout gas of the vampires over him. One whiff of it and the officer's eyes were rolling in their sockets. I caught him as he fell, and gently lowered him to the floor.

"I was not expecting you so soon," Mr. Crepsley said conversationally, picking at the lock of his left handcuff with the fingers of his right.

"We didn't want to keep you waiting," I said tightly, eager to be out of there, but not wanting to appear any less composed than my old friend and mentor, who looked entirely untroubled.

"You should not have rushed on my account," Mr. Crepsley said, his handcuffs snapping free with a click. He bent to work on the chains around his ankles. "I was perfectly content. These are old-style handcuffs. I was wriggling out of their kind before the officers holding me were even born. It was never a question of *if* I was going to escape, but rather *when*."

"He can be an annoying . . . know-it-all some-times," Harkat commented dryly. He'd knocked the guard out and had shuffled over to the table, to make his way back up to the safety of the ceiling.

"We can leave you behind and return for you later," I suggested to the vampire as he stepped out of his leg restraints.

"No," he said. "I might as well depart now that you are here." He winced as he took a step forward. "But, seriously, a few extra hours would not have been unwelcome. My ankle has healed considerably, but is not yet one hundred percent. Further rest would have been beneficial."

"Will you be able to walk?" I asked.

He nodded. "I will win no races, but nor shall I be a hindrance. I am more worried about the sun — I have over two and a half hours of it to deal with."

"We'll cross that bridge when we come to it," I snapped. "Now, are you ready to continue, or do you want to stand here and shoot the breeze all day until the police come back?"

"Nervous?" Mr. Crepsley asked, a glint in his eye.

"Yes," I said.

"Do not be," he told me. "The worst the humans

can do is kill us." He got up on the table and paused. "By the end of the coming night, death may seem a blessing."

With that cheerless comment, he followed Harkat up into the gloomy half-world of the rafters. I waited for him to pull his legs clear, then jumped up after him. We spread out so we weren't in one another's way, then Mr. Crepsley asked which direction we should take.

"Right," I replied. "That leads to the rear of the building, I think."

"Very well," Mr. Crepsley said, wriggling ahead of us. "Crawl slowly," he whispered over his shoulder, "and try not to pick up any splinters."

Harkat and I shared a rueful look — the phrase "cool as a cucumber" could have been invented with Mr. Crepsley in mind — then hurried after the departing vampire before he got too far ahead and left us behind.

CHAPTER EIGHT

WE KICKED OUR WAY through the wall at the back of the building and found ourselves on the second floor, above a deserted alley.

"Can you jump?" I asked Mr. Crepsley.

"No," he said, "but I can climb."

While Mr. Crepsley swung out over the edge of the hole in the wall and dug his nails into the bricks, Harkat and I dropped to the ground and crouched low, scanning the shadows for signs of life. When Mr. Crepsley joined us, we hurried to the end of the alley, where we paused to scout the terrain.

Mr. Crepsley glanced up at the sun. It wasn't very strong — a weak, autumnal, afternoon glow — but two hours of exposure could be fatal for the vampire. If he'd been wearing his cloak, he could have pulled it up over his head and sheltered beneath it, but he'd taken it off in the apartment and left it there.

"What do we do now?" Harkat asked, gazing around uncertainly.

"Find a manhole and get underground," I replied. "They won't be able to track us through the tunnels, and Mr. Crepsley won't have to worry about the sun."

"A worthy plan," Mr. Crepsley said, rubbing his sore right ankle and looking for a manhole cover. There weren't any in the immediate vicinity, so we pressed on, Harkat and I supporting the vampire, sticking close to the walls of the alley.

The alley forked at the end. The left turn led toward a busy main street, the right on to another dark alley. I'd turned right on impulse and was starting toward the alley when Harkat stopped me.

"Wait," he hissed. "I see a way down."

I looked back and saw a cat picking through a mound of garbage that had spilled out of a toppled bin and half-obscured a round manhole cover. Hurrying over, we shooed the cat away — cats aren't great lovers of vampires, and it hissed angrily at us before fleeing — and kicked the garbage from the cover. Then Harkat and I pulled the cover off and laid it to one side.

"I'll go first," I said, starting down the ladder into the welcome darkness. "Mr. Crepsley next. Harkat last."

They didn't question my orders. As a Vampire Prince, it was my place to take control. Mr. Crepsley would have objected if he disagreed with my decision, but in the normal course of things he was satisfied to follow my command.

I climbed down the ladder. The rungs were cold and my fingers tingled from the contact. As I neared the bottom, I stretched out my left leg to step off the ladder —

— then snatched it back quickly when a gun fired and a bullet tore a chunk out of the wall close to the side of my shin!

Heart pounding, I clung to the ladder, ears ringing from the echoes of the bullet, wondering how the police got down here so quickly, and how they knew which way we'd take.

Then someone chuckled in the darkness and said, "Greetings, vampire. We've been expecting you."

My eyes narrowed. That was no policeman — it was a vampet! Despite the danger, I squatted low on the ladder and peered up the tunnel. There was a large man standing in the shadows, too far away for me to identify.

"Who are you?" I snapped.

"One who follows the Lord of the Vampaneze," he answered.

"What are you doing here?"

"Blocking your passage," he chuckled.

"How did you know we'd come this way?"

"We didn't. But we guessed you'd escape and make for the tunnels. Our Lord doesn't want you down here yet — the day is long, and it amuses him to think of you and your vampire friend struggling through it — so we've blocked off all entrances to the underworld. When night falls, we'll retreat, but until then these tunnels are off limits."

With that, he fired at me again. It was a warning shot, like the first, but I didn't stick around to test his aim any further. Climbing the ladder, I shot out of the manhole as though propelled, and cursed loudly as I kicked a large empty can across the alley.

"Police?" Mr. Crepsley asked sullenly.

"No — vampets. They've blocked off all entrances to the tunnels until nightfall. They want us to suffer."

"They can't have covered *every* . . . entrance, can they?" Harkat asked.

"Enough of them," Mr. Crepsley responded. "The tunnels this close to the surface are carefully linked. By choosing the right spot, one man can block the paths of six or seven entrances. If we had time, we might find a way past, but we do not. We must abandon the tunnels."

"Where do we go instead?" I asked.

"We run," the vampire said simply. "Or hobble, as the case may be. We try to avoid the police, find somewhere to hole up, and wait for night."

"That won't be easy," I noted.

Mr. Crepsley shrugged. "If you had held tight for sunset to make your break, it would have been easier. You did not, so we must make the best of things. Come," he said, turning his back on the manhole. "Let us make tracks."

I paused to spit bitterly down the hole, then took off after Mr. Crepsley and Harkat, putting the disappointment of the blocked-off tunnels behind, focusing on the flight ahead.

Less than three minutes later, the police were hot on our trail.

We heard them spilling out of the station, shouting at each other, piling into cars, honking horns, turning blaring sirens on full. We'd been moving steadily but hadn't drifted far away from the station — we'd been avoiding main streets, sticking to back alleys, which had an annoying habit of doubling back on themselves. We'd have taken to the rooftops, except that would have meant exposing Mr. Crepsley more fully to the rays of the sun.

"This is useless," the vampire said as we drew up beside a building overlooking a busy shopping street. "We are making no progress. We must ascend."

"But the sun . . ." I said.

"Forget it," he snapped. "If I burn, I burn. It will not kill me immediately — but the police will if they catch up!"

Nodding, I looked for a way up to the roofs. Then a thought struck. I gazed at the teeming street, then studied my clothes. I was disheveled and dirty, but didn't look a whole lot worse than any average teenager going through a grunge or heavy metal phase.

"Do we have money?" I asked, rubbing the worst of the dirt from my face and slicking back my hair with a handful of spit. Then I tucked the chains of the cuffs in under my shirt ends and pants legs, masking them from view.

"The time he picks to go shopping!" Harkat groaned.

"I know what I'm doing," I grinned. "Do we have money or not?"

"I had some notes, but the police took them," Mr. Crepsley said. "I am . . . how do the humans put it . . . broken?"

"Broke," I laughed. "No matter. I'll do without."

"Wait!" Harkat said as I started forward. "Where are you going? We can't split up . . . now. We must stay together."

"I won't be long," I said. "And I won't take any stupid chances. Wait here for me. If I'm not back in five minutes, leave without me and I'll catch up with you later, in the tunnels."

"Where are you —" Mr. Crepsley began, but I didn't have time for a debate, so I slid out of the alley before he finished and walked swiftly along the street, looking for a grocery store.

I kept one eye peeled for police or soldiers, but there were none around. After a few seconds, I spotted a shop across the street, waited for the light to turn green, then strolled across and entered. A middle-aged woman and a young man with long hair were serving behind the counter. The shop was quite busy — there were six or seven customers — which was good. It meant I wouldn't stick out. A TV on the left of the doorway was tuned to a news channel, but the sound was down low. There was a security camera above the TV, scanning and recording, but that didn't bother me — with all the crimes I'd been charged with, I wasn't going to sweat about being booked for petty theft!

I walked slowly up and down the aisles, looking for sunwear items. It wasn't the right time of year for sunglasses and sun hats, but I was sure they'd have a few knickknacks lying around somewhere.

Next to a row of baby-care products, I found them — several bottles of suntan lotion, standing forlornly on a battered old shelf. The choice wasn't great, but they'd do. I quickly read the labels, looking for the strongest sunblock I could find. SPF ten . . . twelve . . . fifteen. I chose the bottle with the highest number (it was for fair-skinned babies, but I wouldn't tell Mr. Crepsley that!), then stood uncertainly with it in my hand, wondering what to do next.

I wasn't an experienced shoplifter. I'd stolen a few sweets with friends when I was very young, and once swiped a load of golf balls with a cousin of mine, but I'd never enjoyed it and hadn't taken it any further. I was sure my face would give me away if I just pocketed the bottle and tried walking straight out of the shop.

I thought about it for a few seconds, then slyly slipped the bottle inside the waist of my trousers, draped the hem of my shirt over it, grabbed another bottle, turned and marched up to the counter.

"Excuse me," I said to the female assistant as she was serving one of the other customers, "but do you have any Sun Undone lotion?" I'd made the name up, and hoped there wasn't a real brand by that name available.

"Only what's on the shelves," the woman snapped irritably.

"Oh," I smiled. "That's OK. Thanks. I'll put this back."

I was turning when the young, long-haired man said, "Hey! Hold on!" Stomach sinking, I looked back questioningly, getting ready to run. "It wasn't Sunny-dun you wanted, was it?" he asked. "We've got a crate of those somewhere in the back. I could get a bottle if you —"

"No," I interrupted, relaxing. "It was Sun Undone. My mom won't use anything else."

"Suit yourself," he shrugged, no longer interested, turning to deal with another customer.

I walked back to the shelf, laid the bottle on it, and made for the door as casually as I could. I nodded amiably at the young man as I was passing, and he half-waved at me in reply. I had one foot out the door, delighted with myself, when I caught sight of a familiar face on the TV and stopped, dumbstruck.

It was *me*!

The photograph must have been taken this morning, while I was being arrested. I looked pale, haggard, and frightened, my hands cuffed, eyes wary, policemen on either side of me.

Stepping back into the store, I reached up and turned up the volume.

"Hey!" the male attendant grunted. "You can't . . ."

I ignored him and concentrated on what the newsreader was saying.

"— might look harmless, but police are urging the public not to be taken in by his appearance. Darren Shan — or Darren Horston, as he is also known — is a teenager, but he consorts with brutal killers, and may be a killer himself."

My photograph faded, to be replaced by a female newsreader with a grim expression. After a couple of seconds, my photo appeared again, smaller this time, in the upper right hand corner of the screen. Harkat's appeared to the left, and accurate artist's impressions of Mr. Crepsley and Vancha Mach between us.

"To repeat our incredible breaking story," said the newsreader. "Four alleged members of the gang of killers known as the Vampires were cornered by the police this morning. One, Vancha March" — the lines around the drawing of Vancha flashed — "escaped, taking Chief Inspector Alice Burgess hostage. The other three were arrested and detained for questioning, but made a violent break for freedom less than twenty minutes ago, killing or seriously wounding an unspecified number of officers and nurses. They are considered armed and exceedingly dangerous. If spotted, they should not be approached. Instead, call one of the following numbers . . ."

I turned away from the TV, stunned. I should have known the media would go into overdrive about a story this big, but I'd innocently assumed that we had only the police and army to worry about. I'd never stopped to think of city-wide alerts and how they'd affect us.

As I stood, digesting this new turn of events, brooding on the news that we'd been blamed for Steve's murders in the station, the middle-aged lady behind the counter pointed at me and gasped in a high voice, "It's him! The boy! The *killer*!"

Startled, I looked up and saw that every person in the shop was staring at me, their faces twisted with fear and horror.

"It's the one called Darren Shan!" a customer yelled. "They say he killed that girl, Tara Williams — that he drank her blood and ate her!"

"He's a vampire!" a wrinkly old man shrieked. "Someone get a stake! We have to kill him!"

That might have been funny if I'd seen it in a movie — the thought of this little old man driving a stake through a vampire's hardened heart was ludicrous — but I didn't have time to see the funny side of things. Raising my hands to show I wasn't armed, I backed out of the door.

"Derek!" the female assistant shouted at the young man. "Grab the gun and shoot him!"

That was enough for me. Pivoting sharply, I dived out of the door and raced across the road, not stopping for traffic, darting out of the way of cars as they screeched to a halt, ignoring the drivers as they pounded on their horns and yelled abuse after me.

I came to a halt in the mouth of the alley, where a worried Harkat and Mr. Crepsley were waiting. Digging out the bottle of suntan lotion, I tossed it to the vampire. "Spread that on yourself, quick," I gasped, bending over for breath.

"What —" he began to ask.

"Don't argue!" I shouted. "Do it!"

The vampire yanked the top off the bottle and poured half the contents out into his hands, then smeared it over his face and scalp and other exposed areas. He rubbed the lotion in, poured the rest out, rubbed that in too, then tossed the bottle away into the gutter.

"Done," he said.

"We certainly are," I muttered, standing up. "You're not going to believe —"

"There they are!" someone bellowed, cutting me short. "That's them — the Vampires!"

The three of us looked around and I saw the little old wrinkly man from the shop wrestling a large rifle from the long-haired attendant. "Give me that!" he shouted. "I hunted deer when I was younger!"

Tossing his walking stick to one side, the old-timer turned, lifted the rifle with remarkable speed, and fired.

We fell to the ground as the wall above our heads exploded into fragments. The old man fired again, even closer this time. But then he had to pause to re-load. While he was doing that, we jumped to our feet, about-faced, and fled, Mr. Crepsley swinging his in-jured leg forward and backward like a demented Long John Silver.

The crowd behind us paused a moment, torn be-tween fear and excitement. Then, with roars of rage, they grabbed sticks and iron bars and the lids off garbage cans, and surged after us. No longer a mere crowd, but a bloodthirsty *mob*.

CHAPTER NINE

WE TORE AHEAD OF THE MOB to begin with — humans can't match vampires or Little People for speed — but then Mr. Crepsley's right ankle swelled up and his pace dropped steadily.

"No . . . good," he gasped, as we stopped at a corner and rested. "Cannot . . . continue. You must go . . . on without me."

"No," I said instantly. "We're taking you with us."

"I cannot . . . keep up," he snarled, teeth gritted against the pain.

"Then we'll stand and fight," I told him. "But we stick together. That's an order."

The vampire forced a weak smile. "Careful, Darren," he said. "You might be a Prince, but you are still my assistant. I can slap sense into you if I have to."

"That's why I have to keep you with me," I grinned. "You stop me from getting a big head."

Mr. Crepsley sighed and bent to rub the purple flesh around his ankle.

"Here!" Harkat said, and we looked up. The Little Person had pulled down the ladder of an overhead fire escape. "They'll find it hard to follow if . . . we take to the roofs. We must go up."

Mr. Crepsley nodded. "Harkat is correct."

"Will the lotion protect you from the sun?" I asked.

"From the worst of it," he said. "I will be red by sunset, but it should prevent severe burning."

"Then let's go!"

I was first up the ladder, Mr. Crepsley next, Harkat last. The mob poured into the alley as Harkat was drawing his legs up, and those to the fore almost grabbed him. He had to kick hard at their hands to break free, then hurried up after us.

"Let me shoot!" the little old man with the rifle was shouting. "Out of my way! I can take them!" But there were too many people in the alley. It was packed tight and he couldn't raise his rifle to aim.

While the humans squabbled over who would get the ladder, we scrambled up the stairs. Mr. Crepsley moved faster now that he had a railing to lean on for support. He winced as we moved out of the shadows and into direct sunlight, but didn't slow down.

I paused at the top of the fire escape and waited for Mr. Crepsley. As I stood there, feeling more confident than I had a couple of minutes earlier, a helicopter dropped from the sky and someone yelled at me through a megaphone, "Stop where you are or we'll shoot!"

Cursing, I called down to Mr. Crepsley, "Quick! We have to go now or —"

I got no further. Above, a marksman opened fire. The air around me whizzed with bullets, which zinged piercingly off the bars of the fire escape. Screaming wildly, I threw myself down the stairs and collided with Mr. Crepsley and Harkat. If Mr. Crepsley hadn't been holding on so tightly to the rail to ease the pressure on his injured ankle, we might all have gone over the side!

We hurried down a couple of flights, where the marksman couldn't see us, then huddled on a landing, frightened . . . miserable . . . *trapped*.

"They might have to leave . . . to refuel," Harkat said hopefully.

"Sure," I snorted, "in an hour or two!"

"How are the humans below faring?" Mr. Crepsley asked.

I stuck my head over the side and looked down. "The first few have made it to the top of the ladder. They'll be on us in a minute or less."

"We are in a good position to defend ourselves here," the vampire mused. "They will have to attack in small groups. We should be able to push them back."

"Sure," I snorted again, "but what good will that do? A few more minutes and the police and soldiers will arrive. It won't take them long to climb the building opposite and pick us off with their rifles."

"Damned above and damned below," Harkat said, wiping a few beads of green sweat from his round, bald head. "That leaves . . ." He pointed to the window behind us, leading into the building.

"Another trap," I complained. "All the police have to do is surround the building, enter in armed teams, flush us out — and we're finished."

"True," Mr. Crepsley agreed thoughtfully, "but what if they have to fight to get in? And what if we are not there when they arrive?"

We stared at Mr. Crepsley questioningly. "Follow me," he said, sliding the window open and crawling inside. "I have a plan!"

Turning our backs on the advancing humans beneath and the hovering helicopter above, Harkat and I dived through the window and into the hall, where Mr. Crepsley was on his feet and calmly brushing flecks of dirt from this shirt, as though waiting for a bus on a slow Sunday morning.

"Ready?" he asked when we were standing beside him.

"Ready for *what*?" I replied, exasperated.

"Ready to set the cat among the pigeons," he laughed. Striding to the nearest door, he paused a moment, then slammed on it with the flat of his palm. "Vampires!" he bellowed. "Vampires in the building! Everybody out!"

He stepped away, faced us, and started counting. "One. Two. Three. Fo —"

The door burst open and a woman wearing a skimpy nightdress and no shoes raced out into the hallway, screeching and waving her hands above her head.

"Quick!" Mr. Crepsley shouted, taking her arm and pointing her toward the stairs. "Head for the ground floor! We have to get out! We will die if we stay! The vampires are here!"

"Aiiieeee!" she screamed, then ran with astonishing speed for the stairs.

"See?" Mr. Crepsley beamed.

"I see," I smirked.

"Me too," Harkat said.

"Then get busy," Mr. Crepsley said, hopping to the next door, pounding upon it, roaring, "Vampires! Vampires! Beware the living dead!"

Harkat and I ran ahead of him, mimicking his knocks and cries, and within seconds the hallway was jammed with terrified humans, running about directionlessly, knocking one another over, almost flying down the stairs to safety.

As we reached the end of the corridor, I glanced over the railing of the stairway and saw those rushing down the stairs colliding with members of the mob, who'd stormed the building in an attempt to track us through it. Those fleeing couldn't get out, and those chasing us couldn't get in.

Wicked!

"Hurry," Harkat said, slapping my back. "They're coming in by the . . . fire escape."

Looking back, I saw the first of our pursuers poking his head through the window. I turned left and raced up the next corridor with Harkat and Mr. Crepsley, raising a false alarm, emptying the apartments of their human inhabitants, clogging the hallway behind us.

While the mob vanguard clashed with the panicked residents, we turned down another corridor, fled to a fire escape on the opposite side of the building, crawled out, and leaped across to the neighboring block of apartments. We darted through this one, spreading the same warning message, banging on doors, yelling about vampires, causing havoc.

Making our way to the rear of the building, we jumped across to a third apartment block, and again set the humans running in fear for their lives. But when we got to the end of this one, we paused and gazed on the alley below and the sky overhead. There was no sign of the mob, and the helicopter was hovering over the two buildings behind us. We could hear police sirens closing in.

"Now is the time to lose ourselves," Mr. Crepsley said. "The chaos behind us will last a handful of minutes at most. We must make good use of that time."

"Which way do we go?" I asked, scanning the surrounding buildings.

Mr. Crepsley's eyes darted from one building to another, settling on a low-built structure to our right. "There," he pointed. "That looks deserted. We will try it and pray that the luck of the vampires is with us."

There was no fire escape where we were, so we hurried down the stairs at the back of the building and out into the alley. Sticking close to the walls, we crept to the building we'd set our sights on, broke a window to gain entry — no alarms sounded — and found ourselves in an old, abandoned factory.

We stumbled up a couple of floors, then ran as fast as we could to the back. There we discovered the shell of a decrepit apartment building due for demolition. Tearing through the lower floor, we emerged at the far side onto a maze of tight, dark, unpopulated alleys. We paused, ears open for sounds of pursuit. There weren't any.

We shared quick, shaky grins, then Harkat and I wrapped an arm around Mr. Crepsley. He raised his painful right foot and we hobbled forward at a slower pace than before, enjoying our period of respite, but experienced enough to know that we weren't out of the frying pan yet. Not by a long shot.

Through the alleys we fled. We passed a few people, but none paid any attention to us — the afternoon was darkening with heavy clouds, casting the already gloomy alleys into pools of murky shadows. We could see clearly with our advanced eyesight, but to humans we appeared as nothing more than vaguely defined figures in the half-light.

Neither the mob nor the police followed. We could still hear the ruckus they were creating, but it hadn't moved on from the three apartment blocks we'd terrorized. For the time being, we were in the clear.

We stopped outside the back of a supermarket to catch our breath. Mr. Crepsley's right leg was purple up to his knee now and he must have been in immense pain. "We need ice for that," I said. "I could slip into the supermarket and —"

"No!" the vampire barked. "You have already inspired one mob with your shopping antics. We can do very nicely without inciting another."

"I was only trying to help," I grumbled.

"I know," he sighed, "but reckless risks only make matters worse. My injury is not as serious as it looks. A few hours' rest and I will be fine."

"How about these cans?" Harkat asked, tapping a couple of large, black garbage cans. "We could crawl inside and wait . . . for night."

"No," I said. "People use cans like this all the time. We'd be discovered."

"Then where?" Harkat enquired.

"I don't know," I snapped. "Maybe we can find an empty apartment or an abandoned building. We could duck into Debbie's if we were close enough, but we're too far . . ."

I stopped, eyes settling on a street sign across from the supermarket. "Baker's Lane," I muttered, rubbing the bridge of my nose. "I know this place. We've been here before, when we were searching for the vampaneze killers, before we knew about R.V. and Steve."

"We traveled almost everywhere in our search for the killers," Mr. Crepsley commented.

"Yes, but I remember this place because . . . because . . ." I frowned, and then it came to me and I snapped my fingers. "Because Richard lives close by!"

"Richard?" Mr. Crepsley frowned. "Your friend from school?"

"Yes," I said, excited. "His house is only three or four minutes away."

"You think he'd shelter us?" Harkat asked.

"Maybe, if I explain things to him." The others looked uncertain. "Do you have any better ideas?" I challenged them. "Richard's a friend. I trust him. The worst he can do is turn us away."

Mr. Crepsley thought about it a moment, then nodded. "Very well. We will ask him for help. As you say, we have nothing to lose."

Leaving the supermarket, we struck out for Richard's house, and this time I walked with a bounce in my step. I was sure Richard would help. After all, hadn't I saved him on the stairs at Mahler's?

We made it to Richard's in just over four minutes. Wasting no time, we climbed onto the roof and hid in the shadows of a large chimney. I'd seen a light in

Richard's room from the ground, so once I was sure that Harkat and Mr. Crepsley were settled, I crept to the edge of the roof and lowered myself over it.

"Wait," Mr. Crepsley whispered, sliding up beside me. "I will come with you."

"No," I whispered back. "The sight of you might scare him. Let me go alone."

"Very well," he said, "but I will wait outside the window, in case you run into trouble."

I didn't see what sort of trouble I could run into, but Mr. Crepsley had a stubborn look in his eyes, so I simply nodded and swung out over the roof, got a toe-hold, drove my fingernails into the stone of the wall, then climbed down to Richard's room like a spider.

The curtains were drawn, but not all the way, and I was able to see directly into my friend's bedroom. Richard was lying on his bed, a bag of popcorn and a glass of orange juice propped on his chest, watching a rerun of the *Addams Family* on a portable TV set.

Richard was laughing at the antics of the TV freaks, and I had to smile at how oddly fitting it was that he should be watching this when three real freaks of the night had just turned up. Fate has a strange sense of humor.

I thought about knocking on the window, but that might startle him. I studied the simple latch inside the glass, then pointed it out to Mr. Crepsley (who'd scaled down the wall beside me) and raised my eyebrows in a silent question: "Can you open it?"

The vampire rubbed the thumb, index and middle fingers of his right hand together very, *very* swiftly. When he'd produced a strong static charge, he lowered his hand, pointed his fingers at the latch, and made a gentle uplifting motion.

Nothing happened.

The vampire frowned, leaned forward for a closer look, then snorted. "It is made of plastic!" I turned aside to hide a smile. "No matter," Mr. Crepsley said, and cut a small hole in the glass with the nail of his right index finger. It made only a tiny squeaking noise, which Richard didn't hear over the sound of the TV. Mr. Crepsley popped the glass inwards, crooked the latch up with his finger, then swung out of the way and motioned me forward.

Taking a deep breath to steady myself, I pushed the window open and stepped into the room as casually as possible. "Hi, Richard," I said.

Richard's head jerked around. When he realized who it was, his jaw dropped and he began to quiver.

"It's OK," I said, taking a step closer to the bed, raising my hands in a gesture of friendship. "I'm not going to hurt you. I'm in trouble, Richard, and I need your help. I have a nerve to ask, but could you put me and a couple of my friends up for a few hours? We'll hide in the wardrobe or under the bed. We won't be any bother, honestly."

"Vuh-vuh-vuh," Richard stuttered, eyes wide with terror.

"Richard?" I asked, concerned. "Are you OK?"

"Vuh-vuh-*vampire!*" he croaked, pointing a trembling finger at me.

"Oh," I said. "You've heard. Yes, I'm a half-vampire, but it's not what you think. I'm not evil or a killer. Let me call my friends, we'll get comfy, then I'll tell you all about —"

"*Vampire!*" Richard screamed, loudly this time, then turned to face the door of his room and bellowed at the top of his lungs: "Mom! Dad! Vampires! Vampires! Vampires! Vam —"

His cries were cut short by Mr. Crepsley, who swung into the room, darted ahead of me, grabbed the boy by his throat, and breathed sharply over his face. Gas shot up Richard's nose and into his mouth. For a second he struggled, terrified. Then his features relaxed, his eyes closed, and he slumped back on the bed.

"Check the door!" Mr. Crepsley hissed, rolling off the bed, crouching on the floor defensively.

I obeyed immediately, even though Richard's

reaction had left me sick to my stomach. Opening the door a crack, I listened for sounds of Richard's family rushing to investigate his cry. They didn't come. The larger TV set in the living room was turned on and the noise must have masked Richard's shouts.

"It's OK," I said, closing the door. "We're safe."

"So much for friendship," Mr. Crepsley snapped, brushing a few popcorn crumbs from his clothes.

"He was scared witless," I said miserably, staring down at Richard. "We were friends . . . he knew me . . . I saved his life . . . and for all that, he still thought I was here to kill him."

"He believes you are a blood-crazed monster," Mr. Crepsley said. "Humans do not understand vampires. His reaction was predictable. We would have anticipated it and left him alone if we had been thinking clearly."

Mr. Crepsley turned slowly and examined the room. "This would be a good place to hide," he said. "The boy's family will probably not bother him when they see that he is sleeping. There is plenty of space in the wardrobe. I think all three of us could fit."

"No," I said firmly. "I won't take advantage of him. If he'd offered his help — great. But he didn't. He was afraid of me. It'd be wrong to stay."

Mr. Crepsley's expression showed what he thought of that, but he respected my wishes and made for the window without any argument. I was heading after him when I saw that during the brief struggle the popcorn had spilled over the bedsheets, and the glass of orange juice had been knocked over. Stopping to shove the popcorn back into its packet, I found a box of tissues, ripped several free and used them to mop up the worst of the orange juice. I made sure Richard was OK, set the TV to "Pause," bade my friend a silent goodbye, and left quietly, to run once again from the misguided humans who wished to kill me.

CHAPTER TEN

WE TOOK TO THE ROOFTOPS. There were no helicopters nearby, and the shadows of the gloomy afternoon masked us from general view, so it seemed safer to carry on up high, where we could make good time.

Moving carefully but quickly, we aimed for areas far beyond the chaos behind us, where we could hole up until night. For fifteen minutes we leaped and slid from one rooftop to another, unseen by anyone, getting farther and farther away from the humans who were hunting us.

Finally, we came to a crumbling old silo — a building in which grain was once stored. A spiral staircase still ran up the outside, though the lowest section had rotted and crumbled away. Leaping onto the upper half of the stairs from a roof, we climbed to the top, kicked down the locked door and let ourselves in.

Closing the door, we edged further into the silo along a narrow ledge, until we reached a semicircular platform, where we lay down. There were holes and cracks in the roof overhead and the dim light was strong enough for us to see by.

"Do you think we'll be . . . safe here?" Harkat asked, lowering his mask. Streams of green sweat were flooding the scars and stitches of his grey face.

"Yes," Mr. Crepsley said confidently. "They will have to organize a complete search. They dare leave no stone unturned. That will slow them down. It will be morning or later before they make it this far across the city." The vampire shut his eyes and massaged his eyelids. Even doused in suntan lotion, his skin had turned a dark pink color.

"How are you bearing up?" I asked.

"Better than I dared hope," he said, still rubbing his eyelids. "I have the start of an excruciating headache, but now that I am out of the sunlight, perhaps it will subside." He lowered his fingers, opened his eyes, stretched his right leg out and stared grimly at the swollen flesh rising from his ankle to his knee. He'd taken his shoes off earlier, which was a good thing, as I doubt he'd have been able to pry the right shoe loose now. "I only hope *that* subsides too," he muttered.

"Do you think it will?" I asked, studying the ugly bruise.

"Hopefully," he said, rubbing his lower leg gingerly. "If not, we may have to bleed it."

"You mean cut into it to let the blood out?" I asked.

"Yes," he said. "Desperate times call for desperate measures. But we will wait and see — with luck it will improve of its own accord."

While Mr. Crepsley was tending to his ankle, I unwrapped the chains around my wrists and legs and tried picking the locks. Mr. Crepsley had taught me the fundamentals of lock-picking, but I'd never quite got the hang of it.

"Here," he said after a couple of minutes, when he saw I wasn't getting anywhere.

The vampire made quick work of the locks, and seconds later the cuffs and chains were lying in heaps on the floor. I rubbed my freed flesh gratefully, then glanced at Harkat, who was using the hem of his robes to wipe green sweat from his face. "How come they didn't put handcuffs on you?" I asked.

"They did," he replied, "but they took them off . . . once I was inside my cell."

"Why?"

The Little Person's wide mouth split into a hideous

smirk. "They didn't know what I was or . . . what to make of me. They asked if I was in . . . pain, so I said I was. They asked if the handcuffs . . . hurt, so I said they did. So they took them off."

"Just like that?" I asked.

"Yes," he chuckled.

"Lucky beggar," I sniffed.

"Looking like something Dr. Frankenstein . . . threw together has its advantages sometimes," Harkat informed me. "That's also why I was . . . alone. I could see they were uneasy . . . around me, so shortly after they began interviewing . . . me, I told them not to touch me — said I had an . . . infectious disease. You should have seen them . . . run!"

All three of us laughed aloud.

"You should've told them you were a resurrected corpse," I chuckled. "That would have put their minds at rest!"

We relaxed after that and lay back against the wall of the silo, saying little, eyes half-closed, ruminating on the day's events and the night to come. I was thirsty, so after a while I climbed down the interior stairs and went looking for water. I didn't find any, but I did find a few cans of beans on a shelf in one of the front offices. Carrying them up, I cut them open with my nails and Mr. Crepsley and I tucked in. Harkat wasn't hungry — he could go for days on end without food if he had to.

The beans settled nicely in my stomach — cold as they were — and I lay back for an hour, quiet and thoughtful. We weren't in any rush. We had until midnight to rendezvous with Vancha (assuming he made it) and it would take us no more than a couple of hours to march through the tunnels to the cavern where we'd fought the vampaneze.

"Do you think Steve escaped?" I asked eventually.

"I am sure of it," Mr. Crepsley replied. "That one has the luck of a demon, and the cunning to match."

"He killed people — police and nurses — while he was escaping," I said.

Mr. Crepsley sighed. "I did not think he would attack those who helped him. I would have killed him before we were taken into custody if I had known what he was planning."

"How do you think he got to be so vicious?" I asked. "He wasn't like this when I knew him."

"Yes, he was," Mr. Crepsley disagreed. "He just had not grown into his true evil self yet. He was born bad, as certain people are. Humans will tell you that everybody can be helped, that everyone has a choice. In my experience, that is not so. Good people can sometimes choose badness, but bad people cannot choose good."

"I don't believe that," Harkat said softly. "I think good and evil exist . . . in all of us. We might be born leaning more toward . . . one than the other, but the choice is there. It *has* to be. Otherwise, we're mere . . . puppets of fate."

"Perhaps," Mr. Crepsley grunted. "Many see it as you do. But I do not think so. Most are born with the freedom of choice. But there are those who defy the rules, who are wicked from the beginning. Maybe they *are* puppets of fate, born that way for a reason, to test the rest of us. I do not know. But natural monsters do exist. On that point, nothing you say can shake me. And Steve Leonard is one of them."

"But then it isn't his fault," I said, frowning. "If he was born bad, he isn't to blame for growing up evil."

"No more than a lion is to blame for being a predator," Mr. Crepsley agreed.

I thought about that. "If that's the case, we shouldn't hate him — we should pity him."

Mr. Crepsley shook his head. "No, Darren. You should neither hate nor pity a monster — merely fear it, and do all in your power to make an end of it before it destroys you." Leaning forward, he rapped on the hard platform with his knuckles. "But remember," he said sternly. "When we venture down the tunnels tonight, Steve Leonard is not our primary enemy —

the Lord of the Vampaneze is. If the chance to kill Leonard arises, by all means seize it. But if you have to choose between him and the Lord he serves, strike first for the latter. We must put our personal feelings aside and focus on our mission."

Harkat and I nodded in agreement with the vampire, but he wasn't finished. Pointing at me with a long, bony finger, he said, "That also applies to Miss Hemlock."

"What do you mean?" I asked.

"The vampaneze might taunt you with her," he said. "We know they cannot kill us — only their Lord dare cut us down. So they may try to split us up, making it easier for them to capture us. It will hurt, but you must put all thoughts of Debbie aside until the quest to kill the Vampaneze Lord has been settled."

"I don't know if I can do that," I said, eyes downcast.

Mr. Crepsley stared hard at me, then dropped his gaze. "You are a Prince," he said quietly. "I cannot command you. If your heart leads you to Debbie, and it proves impossible to resist its call, you must follow. But I ask you to remember the vampires you serve, and what will happen to our clan if we fail."

I nodded soberly. "I haven't forgotten. I'm just not sure, in the heat of the moment, if I'll be able to abandon her."

"But you know that you should?" he pressed. "You understand how important your choice is?"

"Yes," I whispered.

"That is enough," he said. "I trust you to make the right choice."

I cocked an eyebrow. "You sound more like Seba Nile with every passing year," I commented dryly. Seba was the vampire who'd taught Mr. Crepsley the ways of the clan.

"I will take that as a compliment," he smiled, then lay back, closed his eyes, and rested in silence, leaving me to think about Debbie and the Lord of the Vampaneze, and contemplate the desperate choice I might be called upon to make.

CHAPTER ELEVEN

MR. CREPSLEY'S ankle had improved vastly by the time we left the silo to face our destiny. His flesh was still a nasty shade of purple, but the worst of the swelling had died down. He tested the ankle as little as possible during our trek through the tunnels, but was able to stand unassisted when he had to.

There was no fuss about our descent into the menacing darkness. When the time came, we simply walked down the stairs of the silo, broke out through a boarded-up door, found a manhole, slipped beneath the streets and advanced. We didn't encounter any vampaneze or traps.

We said nothing during the journey. Each of us knew how serious this was, and the odds were stacked against us. Victory was unlikely, and even if it came, escape seemed impossible. If we managed to kill the

Lord of the Vampaneze, his followers would surely cut us down in revenge, their hands no longer tied by the prophecies of Mr. Tiny. We were marching to our doom, and tongues have a tendency to seize up at such times, regardless of how brave you might be.

After a long, uneventful journey, we reached the newly built tunnels, dry and warm in comparison to the older links, and from there it was only a short walk to the cavern where we'd faced the vampaneze less than twenty-four hours ago.

Twenty-four hours . . . It felt like years!

Several burning candles were set in nooks around the walls, and their light revealed an apparently deserted cavern. The bodies of the vampaneze we'd killed the night before had been dragged away, though drying pools of their blood remained. The huge door at the other side of the cavern was closed.

"Tread carefully," Mr. Crepsley said, pausing at the entrance. "Hold your weapons low and —"

He stopped abruptly and his face fell. Clearing his throat, he said in a surprisingly meek voice, "Did either of you bring a weapon?"

"Of course —" I began, then stopped as suddenly as Mr. Crepsley had, my hand flying to my waist, where my sword would normally be nesting. But not now. I'd abandoned it when I was arrested, and with all that had happened since then, it had never occurred to me to replace it.

"Um . . . you're not going to believe this . . . ," I mumbled.

"You forgot too?" Mr. Crepsley groaned.

We looked appealingly at Harkat.

The Little Person shook his neckless grey head. "Sorry."

"Brilliant!" Mr. Crepsley snapped. "The most important fight of our lives, and we come unarmed. What manner of fools are we?"

"The greatest who ever stalked the shadows of the night," said someone from within the cavern.

Freezing, we stared into the gloom, our fingers twitching helplessly by our sides. Then a head popped into view from above the doorway and our hearts sank back in our chests. *"Vancha!"* we cheered.

"The one and only," grinned the Prince. He swung around from where he'd been hanging from the ceiling. Landing on his feet, he turned to greet us. Harkat and I hurried forward and embraced the scruffy, smelly man with the dyed green hair and animal hides. Vancha's huge eyes widened with surprise. Then his small mouth split into a smile. "Sappy idiots," he chuckled, hugging us back. He stuck his arms out to Mr. Crepsley. "Haven't *you* got a hug for me, Larten, old buddy?" he croaked.

"You know where you can insert your hug," Mr. Crepsley retorted.

"Oh, the ingratitude," Vancha moaned, then let us go and took a step back, beckoning us forward into the cavern. "Is it true what I overheard?" he asked. "You came without weapons?"

"We have had a difficult afternoon," Mr. Crepsley sniffed, ears reddening.

"It must have been the most bloody awful afternoon in history if you forgot to come armed to the scrap of the century," Vancha chuckled, then grew serious. "Did you get away OK? Any unpleasantness?"

"Our breakout was relatively easy," Mr. Crepsley said. "There were some sticky moments along the way — it has been a long time since I had to flee a wrathful mob — but all things considered, we fared rather splendidly. Our captors, however, were not so fortunate . . ."

He told Vancha about Steve and the guards and nurses he'd killed. Vancha's red face — he'd been engaged in a private duel with the sun for many decades — darkened when he heard the news. "That one is aptly nicknamed," he growled. "If ever a human was bonded at the soul with a leopard, it's him. I just pray to the gods that I have a chance to slit his throat tonight."

"You'll have to get in line," I said. Nobody laughed — they knew I wasn't joking.

"Anyway," Vancha boomed, "one point of order at a time. I don't mind taking the vampaneze on empty-handed — it's my preferred method of fighting—but you three will need more than your fists and feet if we're to stand any chance of getting out of this alive. Luckily, Uncle Vancha has been busy. Follow me."

Vancha led us to one of the darker corners of the cavern, where a small pile of weapons lay stacked next to a large, motionless figure.

"Where did you get these?" Harkat asked, jumping on the weapons before Mr. Crepsley and I had a chance. Rooting through them, he found a jagged knife and a small double-headed axe, which he swung over his head, delighted.

"The vampaneze left them when they were clearing their dead away," Vancha explained. "I imagine they assumed we'd come armed. If they knew how empty-headed you were, they'd have taken more care."

Ignoring the Prince's jibes, Mr. Crepsley and I picked through the pile. He took a couple of long knives and a few shorter ones for throwing. I found a small curved sword I liked the feel of. I tucked a knife into the back of my pants, for back-up, and then I was ready.

"What's that?" Harkat asked, nodding at the large figure on the ground.

"My guest," Vancha said, and rolled the figure over.

The pale white face of a bound, gagged, enraged Chief Inspector Alice Burgess came into view. "Urfl guffle snurf!" she shouted into the folds of her gag, and I'm certain she wasn't saying hello or wishing us well!

"What's she doing here?" I snapped.

"She was company for me," Vancha smirked. "Besides, I didn't know what to expect when I returned. If the police had taken to the tunnels and sewers, I might have needed her to trade my way past."

"What do you plan to do with her now?" Mr. Crepsley asked coolly.

"I'm not sure," Vancha frowned, crouching to study the Chief Inspector. "I tried explaining things to her while we were passing the day away in a forest a few miles outside the city, but I don't think she believed me. In fact, by what she told me to do with my tales of vampires and vampaneze, I *know* she didn't!" The Prince paused. "Having said that, she'd be a great one to have on our side. We may have need of an extra pair of hands in the battle ahead."

"Could we trust her?" I asked.

"I don't know," Vancha said. "But there's one way to find out."

Vancha started to undo the knots of the Chief Inspector's gag. He stopped on the final knot and addressed her sternly. "I'm only going to say this once, so pay attention. I'm sure your first impulse when I free you will be to scream and curse and tell us what trouble we're in. And when you're on your feet, weapon in hand, you might feel like taking a stab at us and setting off by yourself.

"*Don't!*" His eyes were grim. "I know what you think of us, but you're wrong. We didn't kill your people. We're out to stop the killers. If you want to put an end to the torment, come with us and fight. You have nothing to gain by attacking us. Even if you don't believe that, act as if you do. Otherwise, I'll leave you here, trussed up like a turkey."

"Animal!" the Chief Inspector spat, as Vancha removed her gag. "I'll see you hang for this, all of you. I'll have you shaved bald, smeared with tar, covered with feathers, then set alight as you dangle!"

"Isn't she magnificent?" Vancha beamed, freeing her legs and arms. "She's been like that all afternoon. I think I'm falling in love."

"Savage!" she shouted, and struck out at him.

Vancha caught her arm and held it in midair, his expression grave. "Remember what I said, Alice? I don't want to leave you here, at the mercy of our enemies, but I will if you force me to."

The Chief Inspector glared at him, then turned her head aside, disgusted, and held her tongue.

"Better," Vancha said, letting go. "Now, pick a weapon — two or three if you'd prefer — and get ready. We have an army of darkness to deal with."

The Chief Inspector gazed around at us uncertainly. "You guys are crazy," she muttered. "You really expect me to believe you're vampires, but not killers? That you're here to take on a bunch of . . . what did you call them?"

"Vampaneze," Vancha said cheerfully.

"That these vampaneze are the bad guys and you're here to sort them out, even though there's dozens of them and only four of you?"

"That's about the sum of it," Vancha smirked, "except there's five of us now, which should make all the difference."

"Crazy," she growled, but bent and picked up a long hunting knife, tested it, and gathered together another few knives. "OK," she said, standing. "I don't believe your story, but I'll tag along for the time being. If we run into these vampaneze, and they're all that you say, I'll throw my lot in with you. If we don't . . ." She pointed at Vancha's throat with the largest of her knives and jerked it sharply to one side.

"I love it when you talk threateningly," Vancha laughed, then checked that we were all prepared, pulled his belts of shurikens tight around his chest, and led us forward in search of the vampaneze lair.

CHAPTER TWELVE

WE DIDN'T get very far before running into our first obstacle. The huge door leading out of the cavern was bolted shut and wouldn't open. It was the type of door you find on walk-in safes in banks. There was a long row of combination locks running across the middle, beneath a circular handle.

"I wrestled with this for more than an hour," Vancha said, tapping the row of small lock windows. "Couldn't make head nor tail of it."

"Let me have a look," Mr. Crepsley said, stepping forward. "I am not adept at locks such as these, but I have broken into safes before. I may be able to . . ." He trailed off, studied the locks a minute, then cursed foully and kicked the door.

"Something wrong?" I asked lightly.

"We cannot go this way," he snapped. "It is too intricately coded. We must find a way around."

"Easier said than done," Vancha replied. "I've scoured the cavern for hidden passages and tunnels — didn't find any. This place has been purpose-built. I think this is the only way ahead."

"What about the ceiling?" I asked. "The vampaneze came that way the last time we were down here."

"There are removable panels in the roof of the cavern," Vancha said, "but the space above them is only accessible from down here, not through the tunnel."

"Couldn't we break through the wall . . . around the door?" Harkat asked.

"I tried," Vancha said, nodding at a hole he'd punched out a few meters to our left. "It's steel-lined. *Thick* steel. Even vampires have their limits."

"This doesn't make sense," I grumbled. "They knew we'd come. They *want* us to come. Why strand us here? There must be a way through." I knelt and examined the rows of tiny windows, each of which contained two numbers. "Explain this lock to me," I said to Mr. Crepsley.

"It is a combination lock. Quite straightforward. The dials are down there." He pointed to a series of thin dials beneath the windows. "You twist them clockwise for a higher number, counter-clockwise for a lower number. When the correct numbers have been entered in all fifteen windows, the door will open."

"And each number's different?" I asked.

"I assume so." He sighed. "Fifteen different locks, fifteen different numbers. I could crack the code eventually, but it would take several nights and days."

"It doesn't make sense," I said again, staring at the meaningless numbers in the windows. "Steve helped design this trap. He wouldn't have built something we couldn't get past. There must be . . ." I stopped. The last three windows were blank. I pointed them out to Mr. Crepsley and asked why.

"They must not form part of the code," he said.

"So we've only twelve numbers to worry about?"

He smiled ruefully. "That should save us half a night or so."

"Why twelve?" I thought aloud, then closed my eyes and tried to think as Steve might (not a pleasant experience!). He'd exercised great patience in tricking us and setting us up for a fall, but now that we were close to the end, I couldn't picture him placing a boulder in our path which would take a week to remove. He'd be eager to get at us. The code he picked must be one we'd be able to crack pretty quickly, so it had to be simple, something which looked impossible, but in reality was as plain as . . .

I groaned, then began counting. "Try these numbers as I call them out," I said to Mr. Crepsley, eyes still closed. "Nineteen . . . Twenty . . . Five . . ."

I carried on until I got to "Eighteen . . . Four." I stopped and opened my eyes. Mr. Crepsley spun the last counter counter-clockwise to four. There was a click and the circular handle popped out. Startled, the vampire grabbed it and twisted. It turned easily at his touch and the round door swung open.

Mr. Crepsley, Harkat and Vancha stared at me, awed.

"How . . . ?" Vancha gasped.

"Oh, please!" Alice Burgess snorted. "Isn't it obvious? He just converted the alphabet into numbers, starting with one and finishing with twenty-six. It's the most simplistic code in operation. A child could work it out."

"Oh," Harkat said. "I get it now, A was 1, B was . . . 2, and so on."

"Right," I smiled. "Using that code, I dialed in 'Steve Leopard.' I knew it had to be something easy like that."

"Isn't education wonderful, Larten?" Vancha smirked. "We'll have to attend night classes when this is over."

"Quiet!" Mr. Crepsley snapped, not amused. He

was gazing into the darkness of the tunnel beyond. "Remember where we are and who we are facing."

"You can't talk to a Prince like that," Vancha grumbled, but straightened up and focused on the stretch of tunnel ahead. "Get in line," he said, moving to take the lead. "I'll go first, Harkat second, Alice in the middle, Darren behind, Larten at the rear."

Nobody argued with him. Though I was of equal rank, Vancha was far more experienced, and there was no doubt as to who was in charge.

Entering the tunnel, we advanced. Though the ceiling wasn't high, the tunnel was wide, and we were able to walk quite comfortably. Torches were set in the walls at regular intervals. I looked for tunnels leading off this one, but couldn't see any. We pressed on straight ahead.

We'd gone maybe forty yards when a sharp, clanging noise behind made us jump. Turning swiftly, we saw someone standing by the door we'd just come through. When he stepped forward into the light of the closest torch, hooks held up above his head, we knew instantly who it was — *R.V.!*

"Lady and gentlemen!" he boomed. "Welcome! The proprietors of the Cavern of Retribution wish you well and hope you enjoy your stay. If you have any complaints, please don't hesitate to —"

"Where's Debbie, you monster?" I screamed, trying to shove past Mr. Crepsley. The vampire held me back with a firm arm and shook his head tautly.

"Remember what we discussed in the silo," he hissed.

I struggled a moment, then stepped back and glared at the insane vampaneze, who was jumping from foot to foot, laughing crazily.

"Where is she?" I snarled.

"Not far from here," he chuckled, his voice carrying in the close confines of the tunnel. "Quite close as the crow flies. Closer still as the crow *dies*."

"That's a lousy pun," Harkat shouted.

"I ain't a poet but I don't know it," R.V. tossed back in reply. Then he stopped dancing and stared at us coldly. "Debbie's close, man," he hissed. "And she's alive. But she won't be much longer, not if you don't come with me now, Shan. Leave your rotten friends and surrender yourself to me — I'll let her go. Stay with them and pursue your hateful quest — I'll kill her!"

"If you do . . ." I growled.

"What?" he jeered. "You'll kill me too? You'll have to catch me first, Shanny boy, and that's a lot easier said than done. R.V.'s quick on his feet, yes indeedy, quick as a gazelle."

"He sounds so much like Murlough," Mr. Crepsley

136

whispered, referring to a mad vampaneze we'd killed many years earlier. "It is as if his spirit has survived and found a home inside R.V."

I had no time to worry about spirits of the past. As I thought over the offer, R.V. darted to a hole on his left — it had been covered by a panel when we passed it — ducked into it, then stuck his head out, grinning wildly. "How about it, Shanny? Your life for Debbie's. Is it a deal or do I make her squeal?"

This was my moment of truth. I'd have given my life gladly if it meant sparing Debbie's. But if the Lord of the Vampaneze got the better of us, he'd lead his people to victory over the vampires. My duty was to those who'd placed their faith in me. I had more than myself to think about. And though it pained me intensely, I lowered my head in response to R.V.'s offer and said softly, "No."

"What was that?" R.V. shouted. "Speak up — I can't hear you."

"*NO!*" I roared, whipping out my knife and launching it at him, although I knew I couldn't hit him from where I was standing.

R.V.'s face twisted with hate. "Cretin!" he snarled. "The others said you wouldn't trade for her, but I was sure you would. Very well. Have it your way, man. It's Debbie stew for breakfast!"

Laughing at me, he withdrew and slammed the panel shut on the passageway. I wanted to run after him, pound on the panel and scream for him to bring Debbie back. But I knew he wouldn't, so I restrained myself — just.

"You did well, Darren," Mr. Crepsley said, laying a hand on my shoulder.

"I did what had to be done," I sighed, taking no pleasures from his compliment.

"Was that one of those vampaneze you've been talking about?" Burgess asked, visibly shaken.

"That's one of our ruby-lipped boys, sure enough," Vancha replied chirpily.

"Are they all like that?" she asked, eyes wide, white hair frizzy with fright.

"Oh, no," Vancha said, faking an innocent look. "Most are far worse!"

Then the Prince winked, faced front, and moved on, leading us further down the throat-like tunnel, into the stomach of the vampaneze's monstrous trap, where destiny and death were lying in wait.

CHAPTER THIRTEEN

THE TUNNEL ran straight and downward for five or six hundred yards, before opening out on to a huge, man-made cavern with smooth walls and an extremely high ceiling. Three heavy silver chandeliers hung from the ceiling, each adorned with dozens of thick, red, burning candles.

As we entered the cavern I saw that it was oval in shape, wide across the middle, narrowing at either end. There was a platform set close in front of the wall across from us, suspended on sturdy steel pillars, fifty feet high. We drifted toward it, weapons poised, spreading out to form an orderly line, Vancha slightly in front, his eyes flicking left, right, upward, searching for vampaneze.

"Hold it," Vancha said as we approached the plat-form. We stopped instantly. I thought he'd seen a vampaneze, but he was gazing down at the ground, puzzled but not alarmed. "Have a look at this," he murmured, beckoning us forward.

Stepping up beside him, I felt my insides turn to ice. We were standing on the edge of a pit — oval like the cavern — which was filled with steel-tipped stakes eight or ten feet tall. It reminded me of the pit in the Hall of Death in Vampire Mountain, only this was much bigger.

"A trap for us to fall . . . into?" Harkat asked.

"I doubt it," Vancha said. "The vampaneze would have covered it over if they wanted us to walk into it." He looked up. The platform was built directly over the pit, the support pillars rising from among the stakes. Now that we were close, we could see a long plank connecting the rear right of the platform to a hole in the wall behind it. There was also a thick rope running from the front left side of the platform to our side of the pit, where it was tied to a large holding stake.

"Looks like that's the only way forward," I noted, not liking the set-up one little bit.

"We could skirt the pit and climb the wall," Mr. Crepsley suggested.

Vancha shook his head. "Look again," he said.

I peered closely at the wall, as did Mr. Crepsley. He

saw what we were looking for just before I did and growled something foul beneath his breath.

"What is it?" Harkat asked, his round green eyes not as sharp as ours.

"There are scores of tiny holes in the wall," I said. "Ideal for firing darts or bullets through."

"They'd cut us down in seconds if we tried climbing it," Vancha said.

"That's dumb," Chief Inspector Burgess muttered. We looked back at her. "Why lay a trap here and not in the tunnel?" she asked. "The walls of the tunnel could have been peppered with holes like that one. We had nowhere to turn, nowhere to run. We were sitting ducks. Why leave it till now?"

"Because it isn't a trap," Vancha told her. "It's a warning. They don't want us going that way. They want us to use the platform."

The police chief frowned. "I thought they wanted to kill you."

"They do," Vancha said, "but they want to play with us first."

"Dumb," she muttered again, clutching her knife close to her chest, turning slowly to survey the whole of the cavern, as though she expected demons to dart from the walls and floor.

"You smell that?" Mr. Crepsley asked, his nose wrinkling.

"Petrol," I nodded. "It's coming from the pit."

"Perhaps we should move back," Vancha suggested, and we quickly withdrew without need of further prompting.

We examined the rope tethered to the stake. It was thickly woven and taut, professionally tied. Vancha tested it by crawling a few yards along, while we stood with our weapons drawn, covering him.

The Prince looked thoughtful when he returned. "It's strong," he said. "I think it would support all of us at the same time. But we won't chance it. We'll cross one at a time, the same order as we came through the tunnel."

"What about the platform?" Harkat asked. "It could be rigged to . . . collapse when we are on it."

Vancha nodded. "When I get up, I'll hurry to the opening across the plank. Don't come up until I'm safe. When you do, make straight for the tunnel. The same goes for the rest of you. If they take the platform down while we're crossing, only one of us will die."

"Great," the Chief Inspector snorted. "So I have a five to one chance of making it across alive."

"Those are good odds," Vancha said. "Much better than those we'll be facing when the vampaneze make their move."

Vancha made sure his shurikens were strapped tight, grabbed hold of the rope, shimmied up it seven feet, then swung over onto his back, so he was hanging upside down. He started across, hand over hand, foot over foot. The rope cut up at a steep angle, but the Prince was strong and his pace didn't falter.

He was almost halfway across, dangling over the pit of deadly stakes, when a figure appeared in the mouth of the tunnel. Burgess spotted it first. "Hey!" she shouted, raising a hand to point. "Someone's up there!"

Our eyes — and Vancha's — snapped to the tunnel entrance. The light was poor, and it was impossible to tell if the figure was big or small, male or female. Then it stepped forward onto the plank and the mystery was solved.

"*Steve!*" I hissed, eyes filling with hatred.

"Howdy, boys!" the half-vampaneze boomed, striding across the plank, not in the least bit afraid of falling and impaling himself on the stakes beneath. "Find your way here OK? I was expecting you ages ago. Thought you might have got lost. I was preparing a search party to send after you."

Steve reached the platform and walked to the waist-high railing that ran around the sides. He peered down at Vancha and beamed as though welcoming an old friend. "We meet again, Mr. March," he chuckled, waving sarcastically.

Vancha snarled like an animal and began crawling faster than before. Steve watched, amused, then reached into a pocket, produced a match and held it up for our eyes to fix on. He winked, bent and struck the match on the floor of the platform. He cupped it close to his face a moment, while it flared into life, then casually tossed it over the railing — into the petrol-soaked pit.

There was an explosive roar which almost burst my eardrums. Flames shot up out of the pit like huge, fiery fingers. They billowed over the edges of the platform, but didn't threaten Steve — he laughed through the red and yellow wall of fire. The flames scorched the roof and wall to the rear — and completely consumed the rope and Vancha, swallowing the prince whole in the blink of a flame-filled eye.

CHAPTER FOURTEEN

I DARTED forward impulsively when I saw Vancha disappear amid the flames, but was quickly forced back by the waves of fire that rolled down toward me. As they broke upon the floor of the cavern, or spat themselves out in the air above our heads, the sound of Steve Leopard's laughter filled my ears. Shielding my eyes with my hands, I glanced up at the platform and saw him leaping about, a heavy sword held high above his head, cheering and whooping with wicked glee. "Bye-bye, Vancha!" he hollered. "So long, Mr. March! Adios, Princey! Farewell, vam —"

"Don't write my death-notices yet, Leonard!" a voice roared from within the blanket of fire, and as Steve's face dropped, the flames died down slightly, revealing a singed, blackened, but very much alive Vancha March, hanging by one hand from the rope, furiously slapping out flames in his hair and animal hides with the other.

"Vancha!" I yelled, delighted. "You're alive!"

"Of course I am," he replied, grinning painfully as he extinguished the last of the flames.

"You're a tough old badger, aren't you?" Steve remarked sourly, glaring down at the Prince.

"Aye," Vancha growled, a gleam in his eye. "And you haven't seen anything yet — just wait till I get my hands on your scrawny, evil neck!"

"I'm *soooo* scared," Steve snorted. Then, as Vancha began climbing again, he hurried to the end of the platform where the rope was tied and tapped it with his sword. "No you don't," he chortled. "One more inch and I'll send you crashing to your doom."

Vancha stopped and studied Steve and the stretch of rope left to cross, calculating the odds. Steve chuckled dryly. "Come off it, March. Even an oaf like you knows when he's beaten. I don't want to cut this rope — not yet — but if I set my mind to it, there's nothing you can do to stop me."

"We'll see about that," Vancha growled, then ripped a throwing star loose and sent it flying at the half-vampaneze.

Steve didn't flinch as the shuriken buried itself harmlessly in the underbelly of the steel platform. "The angle isn't right," he yawned, unimpressed. "You can't hit me from there, no matter how fine a shot you are. Now, will you slide down and join your friends on the ground, or do I have to get nasty?"

Vancha spat at Steve — his spit falling far short of its target — then tucked his arms and legs around the rope and quickly slid over the heads of the flames, away from the platform, to where we were waiting.

"Wise move," Steve said as Vancha steadied himself on his feet and we checked his back and hair for smoldering embers.

"If I had a gun," Burgess muttered, "I could take that wise guy out."

"You're starting to see things from our point of view," Vancha noted wryly.

"I'm still undecided about you lot," the Chief Inspector replied, "but I know out-and-out evil when I see it."

"Now then," Steve announced loudly, "if we're all good and ready, let's get this show on the road." Sticking two fingers between his lips, he whistled loudly three times. Above us, panels in the ceiling were ripped free, and vampaneze and vampets descended on ropes. Similar panels were removed in the walls of the cavern and more of our enemies stepped through and advanced. I counted twenty . . . thirty . . . forty . . . more. Most were armed with swords, axes and clubs, but a few of the vampet carried rifles, handguns and crossbows.

We backed up to the edge of the pit as the vampaneze and vampets closed on us, so they couldn't attack us from behind. We stared at the ranks of grim-face soldiers, counting silently, hopes fading as we realized how hopelessly overwhelmed we were.

Vancha cleared his throat. "I make it about ten or twelve for each of us," he commented. "Does anybody have any favorites, or will we divide them up at random?"

"You can take as many as you want," I said, spotting a familiar face in the middle of the crowd to my left, "but leave that guy over there for me."

Chief Inspector Burgess gasped when she saw who I was pointing at. *"Morgan James?"*

"Evening, ma'am," the sharp-eyed policeman/vampet saluted her mockingly. He'd changed out of his uniform. He was now wearing the brown shirt and black pants of the vampets, and he'd daubed red circles of blood around his eyes.

"Morgan's one of *them*?" the Chief Inspector asked, shocked.

"Yes," I said. "He helped me escape. He knew that Steve would murder his colleagues — and he let him."

Her face darkened. "Shan," she growled, "if you

want him, you'll have to fight me for him — that bastard's *mine*!"

I turned to argue with her, saw the fierce glow in her eyes, and relented with a nod.

The vampaneze and vampets stopped about ten feet short of us and stood, swinging their weapons, eyes alert, awaiting the order to attack. On the platform, Steve grunted happily, then clapped his hands. Out of the corner of my eye I saw somebody appear in the mouth of the tunnel behind us. Glancing over my shoulder, I realized two people had emerged and were crossing the plank to the platform. Both were familiar — Gannen Harst and the Lord of the Vampaneze!

"Look!" I hissed at my companions.

Vancha moaned aloud when he saw the pair, turned quickly, drew three of his shurikens, took aim and fired. The range wasn't a problem, but the angle — as when he was on the rope and firing at Steve — wasn't favorable, and the stars struck and bounced off the underside of the platform.

"Greetings, brother," Gannen Harst said, nodding at Vancha.

"We've got to get up there!" Vancha snapped, looking for a way forward.

"If you can lead, I will gladly follow," Mr. Crepsley said.

"The rope . . . ," Vancha began, but stopped when he saw a group of vampaneze standing between us and the stake where the rope was tied. Even the wild, ever-optimistic Prince knew there was no way through so many foes. If the element of surprise had been on our side, we might have battled through them, but after our last encounter they were prepared for mindless, lightning attacks.

"Even if we made the . . . rope," Harkat said, "those on the platform could cut it before . . . we got across."

"So what do we do?" Vancha growled, frustrated.

"*Die?*" Mr. Crepsley suggested.

Vancha winced. "I don't fear death," he said, "but I won't rush to embrace it. We aren't finished yet. We wouldn't be standing here talking if we were — they'd have rushed us by now. Cover me." So saying, he turned to address the trio on the platform, who were now standing side by side, close to the plank.

"Gannen!" Vancha shouted. "What's going on? Why haven't your men attacked us yet?"

"You know why," Harst responded. "They're afraid they might kill you in the heat of battle. According to Desmond Tiny, only our Lord is supposed to kill the hunters."

"Does that mean they won't defend themselves if we attack?" Vancha asked.

Steve barked a laugh. "Dream on, you stupid old —"

"Enough!" Gannen Harst shouted, silencing the half-vampaneze. "You will not interrupt when I am speaking with my brother." Steve glowered at the protector of the Vampaneze Lord, then lowered his head and held his tongue.

"Of course they'll defend themselves," Harst said, facing Vancha again, "but we hope to avoid such a scene. Apart from the risk of killing you, we've lost too many good men already and don't wish to sacrifice any more. It might be possible to reach a compromise."

"I'm listening," Vancha said.

Gannen Harst gave Steve a quick look. Steve cupped his hands to his mouth and shouted at the ceiling, "Lower away, R.V.!"

There was a pause, then a panel in the ceiling was thrown back and somebody was lowered through the gap on a rope — *Debbie!*

My heart lurched at the sight of her, and I raised my arms, as though I could reach across the great divide and grab her. She didn't appear to have suffered at the hands (*hooks*) of the insane R.V., though her forehead was gashed, her clothes were ripped, and she looked incredibly weary. Her hands were tied behind her back, but her legs were free, and she kicked out at Steve and the others as she came level with the platform. They only laughed, and R.V. lowered her another few feet, so she was too low to aim at them.

"Debbie!" I shouted desperately.

"Darren!" she screamed. "Get out! Don't trust them! They let Steve and R.V. do as they please. They even take orders from them. Flee quick before —"

"If you don't shut up," Steve snarled, "I'll shut you up." He stretched the flat of his sword out and touched it to the thin rope tied around her middle — which was all that lay between Debbie and a deadly drop into the pit.

Debbie saw the peril she was in and bit down on her tongue.

"Good," Gannen Harst said when silence had returned. "Now — our offer. We are interested only in the hunters. Debbie Hemlock, Alice Burgess, and the Little Person don't matter. We have you outnumbered, Vancha. Our victory is assured. You cannot win, only injure us, and perhaps foil us by dying at the hands of one who isn't our Lord."

"That'll be good enough for me," Vancha sniffed.

"Perhaps," Harst nodded. "And I'm sure Larten Crepsley and Darren Shan feel the same. But what of the others? Will they give their lives so freely, for the sake of the vampire clan!"

"I will!" Harkat boomed.

Gannen Harst smiled. "I expect you would, grey one. But you don't have to. Nor do the women. If Vancha, Larten, and Darren lay down their weapons and surrender, we'll free the rest of you. You can walk away, lives intact."

"No way!" Vancha shouted immediately. "I wouldn't roll over and die at the best of times — I'm certainly not doing it now, when so much is at stake."

"Nor shall I agree to such a deal," Mr. Crepsley said.

"What of Darren Shan?" Harst asked. "Will he agree to our deal, or will he condemn his friends to die with the rest of you?"

All eyes fixed on me. I gazed up at Debbie, dangling on the rope, frightened, bloodied, desolate. I had it in my power to set her free. Cut a deal with the vampaneze, face a quick death instead of perhaps a slow, painful one, and save the life of the woman I loved. It would have been inhuman of me to reject such a deal . . .

. . . but I *wasn't* human. I was a half-vampire. More — a Vampire Prince. And Princes don't cut deals, not when the fate of their people is at stake. "No," I said miserably. "We fight and we die. All for one and one for all."

Gannen Harst nodded understandingly. "I expected that, but one should always open with a weak offer. Very well — let me put another proposal to you. Same basic outline as the first. Drop your weapons, surrender, and we let the humans walk. Only this time, Darren Shan gets to go head to head with our Lord and Steve Leonard."

Vancha's face creased suspiciously. "What are you talking about?"

"If you and Larten turn yourselves over to us without a fight," Harst said, "we will allow Darren to duel with our Lord and Steve Leonard. It will be two on one, but he'll be equipped with weapons. If Darren wins, we free all three of you along with the others. If he loses, we execute you and Larten, but the humans and Harkat Mulds go free.

"Think it over," he urged us. "It's a good, honest deal, more than you could have reasonably hoped for."

Vancha turned away from the platform, troubled, and looked to Mr. Crepsley for advice. The vampire, for once, didn't know what to say, and merely shook his head mutely.

"What do *you* think?" Vancha asked me.

"There has to be a catch," I muttered. "Why risk their Lord's life if they don't have to?"

"Gannen wouldn't lie," Vancha said. His face hardened. "But he mightn't tell us the whole truth. Gannen!" he roared. "What guarantee do you give that it'll be a fair fight? How do we know that R.V. or the others won't join in?"

"I give my word," Gannen Harst said softly. "Only the pair on the platform with me will fight Darren Shan. Nobody else will interfere. I'll kill any who seeks to swing the balance one way or the other."

"That's good enough for me," Vancha said. "I believe him. But is this the way we want to go? We've never seen their Lord fight, so we don't know what he's capable of — but we know Leonard's a sly, dangerous opponent. The two of them together . . ." He grimaced.

"If we agree to Gannen's deal," Mr. Crepsley said, "And send Darren up to face them, we place all our eggs in one basket. If Darren wins — wonderful. But if he loses . . ."

Mr. Crepsley and Vancha gazed long and hard at me.

"Well, Darren?" Mr. Crepsley asked. "It is an enormous burden to take upon yourself. Are you prepared to shoulder such a solemn responsibility?"

"I don't know," I sighed. "I still think there's a catch. If the odds were fifty-fifty, I'd jump at it. But I don't think they are. I believe . . ." I stopped. "But that doesn't matter. If this is our best chance, we have to grab it. If you two trust me, I'll accept the challenge — and the blame if I fail."

"He said that like a true vampire," Vancha noted warmly.

"He *is* a true vampire," Mr. Crepsley replied, and I felt pride bloom burningly within me.

"Very well," Vancha shouted. "We accept. But first you have to set the humans and Harkat free. After that, Darren fights your Lord and Steve. Only then, if the fight is fair and he loses, will Larten and I lay down our arms."

"That's not the deal," Harst replied stiffly. "You must lay your weapons to one side and surrender before —"

"No," Vancha interrupted. "We do it this way or not at all. You have my word that we'll let your people take us if Darren loses — assuming he loses fairly. If my word's not good enough, we have a problem."

Gannen Harst hesitated, then nodded curtly. "Your word is good," he said, then told R.V. to haul Debbie up and escort her down.

"No!" R.V. howled. "Steve said I could kill her! He said I could cut her up into tiny little pieces and —"

"Now I'm saying different!" Steve roared. "Don't

cross me on this. There'll be other nights and humans — plenty of them — but there's only one Darren Shan."

We heard R.V. grumbling, but then he pulled on the rope and Debbie ascended in a series of short, uncomfortable jerks.

While waiting for Debbie to be returned to us, I got ready for my fight with the pair on the platform, wiping my hands clean, checking my weapons, clearing my mind of all thoughts except those of battle.

"How do you feel?" Vancha asked.

"Fine."

"Remember," he said, "all that matters is the result. Fight dirty if you have to. Kick and spit, scratch and pinch, hit below the belt."

"I will," I grinned. Lowering my voice, I asked, "Will you really surrender if I lose?"

"I gave my word, didn't I?" Vancha said, then winked and whispered in a voice even lower than mine. "I promised we'd drop our weapons and let them take us. And so we will. But I said nothing about letting them keep us or not picking our weapons up again!"

The vampaneze ahead of us parted ranks as R.V. marched through, dragging Debbie behind him by her hair.

"Stop that!" I shouted angrily. "You're hurting her!"

R.V. bared his teeth and laughed. He was still wearing one red contact lens and hadn't replaced the one he'd lost the night before. His bushy beard was flecked with bits of moss, twigs, dirt and blood. It would have been easy to feel sorry for him — he'd been a decent man before he lost his hands to the jaws of the Wolf-Man at the Cirque Du Freak — but I had no time for sympathy. I reminded myself that he was the enemy and erased all traces of pity from my mind.

R.V. tossed Debbie down in front of me. She cried out in pain, then lunged to her knees and flew into my arms. I clutched her close as she sobbed and tried to speak. "Shhh," I said. "Take it easy. You're safe. Don't say anything."

"I . . . must," she wept. "So much . . . to say. I . . . I love you, Darren."

"Of course you do," I smiled, my eyes filling with tears.

"Such a touching scene," Steve sneered. "Someone pass me a hankie."

I ignored him and held Debbie's face away from me. I kissed her quickly, then smiled. "You look awful," I said.

"Charming!" she half-laughed, then stared at me appealingly. "I don't want to leave," she croaked. "Not until after the fight."

"No," I said quickly. "You have to go. I don't want you to stay and watch."

"In case you are killed?" she asked.

I nodded, and her lips thinned almost to nothing.

"I want to stay too," Harkat said, stepping up beside us, his green eyes filled with determination.

"It's your right to," I agreed. "I won't stop you. But I'd rather you didn't. If you value our friendship, you'll take Debbie and the Chief Inspector, lead them to the surface, and make sure they get away safely. I don't trust these monsters — they might go on a rampage and kill us all if I win."

"Then I should stay to fight . . . with you," Harkat said.

"No," I said softly. "Not this time. Please, for my sake and Debbie's, will you leave?"

Harkat didn't like it, but he nodded reluctantly.

"Come on then," someone snapped behind us. "Let's get them out if they're going."

I looked up and saw the treacherous police officer called Morgan James striding toward us. He was carrying a slim rifle, the butt of which he poked into his Chief Inspector's ribs.

"Get the hell away from me!" she snapped, turning on him furiously.

"Easy, Chief," he drawled, grinning like a jackal, bringing up the rifle. "I'd hate to have to shoot you."

"When we get back, you're history," she snarled.

"I won't be coming back," he smirked. "I'll guide you lot to the cavern at the end of the tunnel, lock you out to make sure you can't create a disturbance, then take off with the others when the fighting's over."

"You won't escape that easy," Burgess snorted. "I'll track you down and make you pay for this, even if I have to travel halfway round the world."

"Sure you will," Morgan laughed, then nudged her in the ribs again, harder this time.

The Chief Inspector spat at her ex-officer, then pushed him away and crouched next to Vancha to tie her laces. As she was doing that, she whispered to him out of the side of her mouth. "The guy in the hood and cloak — that's the one you have to kill, right?" Vancha nodded wordlessly, guarding his expression. "I don't like the idea of sending the kid up to fight them," Burgess said. "If I can create a bit of space, and provide firing cover, d'you reckon you or Crepsley could get up there?"

"Maybe," Vancha said, lips barely moving.

"Then I'll see what I can do." Burgess finished tying her laces, stood and winked. "Come on," she said aloud to Harkat and Debbie. "The air stinks here. The sooner we're out, the better."

The Chief Inspector started walking, shoving ahead of Morgan, purpose in her stride. The rows of vampaneze ahead of her parted, clearing a path. Only a few now stood between us and the stake the rope was tied to.

Harkat and Debbie looked back at me sorrowfully. Debbie opened her mouth to say something, but words wouldn't come. Crying, she shook her head and turned her back on me, shoulders shaking miserably. Harkat put his arms around her and led her away, following the Chief Inspector.

Burgess was almost at the mouth of the tunnel leading out of the cavern when she paused and glanced over her shoulder. Morgan was close to her, cradling his rifle. Harkat and Debbie were several yards behind, progressing slowly.

"Hurry up!" Burgess snapped at the dawdling pair. "This isn't a funeral procession!"

Morgan smiled and looked back automatically at Harkat and Debbie. As he did, the Chief Inspector swung into action. Throwing herself at him, she grabbed the butt of the rifle and dug it into the soft flesh of his stomach, fast and hard, winding him. Morgan yelled in pain and surprise, then snatched the rifle back as she tried to pull it away. He almost wrenched it from her grasp, but not quite, and the pair rolled over on the ground, wrestling for the gun. Behind them, the vampaneze and vampets moved to intercept them.

Before the advancing troops reached her, Burgess got a finger on the trigger of the rifle and squeezed off a shot. It could have been pointing anywhere — she didn't have time to aim — but as luck had it, it was pointing at the jaw of the vampet she was struggling with — Morgan James!

There was a flash and a roar of gunfire. Then Morgan was falling away from the Chief Inspector, shrieking with agony, the left side of his face a bloody, shredded mess.

As Morgan surged to his feet, hands clutching the remains of his face, Burgess slammed him over the back of his head with the butt of the rifle, knocking him unconscious. Then, as vampaneze and vampets swarmed towards her, she leaned a knee on the ex-officer's back, swung her rifle up, took careful aim, and fired off a volley of shots at the platform — at Steve, Gannen Harst . . . and the Lord of the Vampaneze!

CHAPTER FIFTEEN

BULLETS POUNDED the platform, railing, wall and ceiling. The three men caught in the line of fire ducked backward quickly, but not quickly enough — one of the bullets struck the Vampaneze Lord high in his right shoulder, drawing an arc of blood and a sharp cry of pain!

At their Lord's cry, the vampaneze and vampets exploded with rage. Screaming and howling like mad animals, they launched themselves *en masse* at the Chief Inspector, who was still firing. Barreling over one another in their haste to be first upon her, they descended upon Burgess in a vicious, churning wave, breaking over Harkat and Debbie along the way.

My first instinct was to rush to Debbie and pull her from the crush, but Vancha grabbed me before I could move and pointed to the rope — it was no longer guarded. I knew immediately that this was our first priority. Debbie would have to fend for herself.

"Who goes?" I gasped, as we hurried to the stake.

"Me," Vancha said, grabbing the rope.

"No," Mr. Crepsley disagreed, laying a hand on the Prince's shoulder. "It must be me."

"We don't have time to —" Vancha started.

"That is true," Mr. Crepsley interrupted. "We do not have time. So let me pass without any arguments."

"Larten . . . ," Vancha growled.

"He's right," I said softly. "It has to be him."

Vancha gaped at me. "Why?"

"Because Steve was my best friend and Gannen's your brother," I explained. "Mr. Crepsley's the only one who can concentrate wholly on the Vampaneze Lord. You or I would have one eye on Steve or Gannen, no matter how hard we tried to ignore them."

Vancha thought about that, nodded and let go of the rope, clearing the way for Mr. Crepsley. "Give them hell, Larten," he said.

"I will." Mr. Crepsley smiled. He took hold of the rope and started across.

"We must cover him from this side," Vancha said, drawing a handful of shurikens and squinting up at the platform.

"I know," I said, eyes on the thrashing vampaneze

ahead of me, ready to combat them when they awoke to the threat of Mr. Crepsley's challenge.

One of the trio on the platform must have spotted Mr. Crepsley, because Vancha suddenly let fly with a couple of throwing stars — he had a clear shot at them from where we were standing — and I heard a curse above as whoever it was jumped back out of the way of the shurikens.

There was a pause, then a roar which filled the cavern and cut through the cries and mayhem of the battling vampaneze. "Servants of the night!" Gannen Harst bellowed. "Look to your Lord! Danger approaches!"

Heads turned and eyes fixed, first on the platform, then on the rope and Mr. Crepsley. With fresh yelps and gasps, the vampaneze and vampets spun and rushed toward the spot where Vancha and I were standing.

If there hadn't been quite so many, they'd have mown us down, but their numbers worked against them. Too many attacked at the same time, resulting in confusion and chaos. So, instead of facing a solid wall of warriors, we were able to pick off individuals.

As I swung my sword wildly and Vancha lashed out with his hands, I spotted Gannen Harst stealing toward the end of the platform where the rope was tied, a sharp dagger in his right hand. It didn't take a genius to work out his intentions. I roared at Vancha, warning him, but there was no room for him to turn and throw. I shouted at Mr. Crepsley to hurry up, but he was still a long way from safety and could go no faster than he was already going.

As Harst reached the rope and prepared to cut it, someone fired at him. He ducked low and rolled back out of the way as bullets turned the air red around him.

Standing on my toes, I spotted a bruised, battered, but still living Alice Burgess, on her feet, rifle in hand, quickly reloading it with bullets she'd snatched from Morgan James. Just ahead of her stood Harkat Mulds and Debbie Hemlock; Harkat wielding his axe, Debbie awkwardly swinging a short sword, both of them protecting the Chief Inspector from the handful of vampaneze and vampets who hadn't been drawn away to deal with the rope.

I felt like cheering aloud at the sight, and would have if a vampaneze hadn't crashed into my back and knocked me to the ground. As I rolled away from stomping feet, the vampaneze dived after me. Pinning me to the floor, he wrapped his fingers around my neck and squeezed. I lashed out at him but he had the best of me — I was finished!

But the luck of the vampires was on my side. Before his fingers could close and crush my throat, one of his own men was punched by Vancha, fell back, collided with the vampaneze on top of me, and knocked him off. As he yelled, frustrated, I leaped to my feet, grabbed a mace that someone had dropped in the fighting, and let him have it full in the face. The vampaneze dropped, screaming, and I was back in the thick of the fighting.

I saw a vampet swing an axe at the rope tied to the stake. Roaring, I threw the mace at him, but too late — the head of the axe cut clean through the strands of the rope, severing it entirely.

My eyes darted to where Mr. Crepsley was hanging, and my insides clenched as he swung down underneath the platform, through the red flames of the pit, which still burned brightly.

It seemed to take an age for the rope to reach the length of its arc and swing back toward me. When it did, the vampire was no longer in sight, and my heart dropped. Then my eyes slid down and I realized he was still clinging to the rope, but had slipped several feet. As flames licked the undersides of his feet, he began climbing again, and within a couple of seconds was clear of the fire and back on course for the platform.

A quick-minded vampet broke clear of the mêlée,

raised a crossbow, and fired at Mr. Crepsley. He missed. Before he could fire again, I found a spear and sent it soaring. It struck him in the upper right arm and he fell to his knees, moaning.

I glanced to where Burgess was firing again, covering Mr. Crepsley as he climbed. Debbie was struggling with a vampet twice her size. She'd thrown her arms around him so he couldn't use his sword and had buried a knife in the small of his back. She was raking his face with her nails, and putting her left knee to very naughty use. Not bad for an English teacher!

Harkat, meanwhile, was chopping vampaneze and vampets to pieces. The Little Person was an experienced, lethal fighter, much stronger and faster than he looked. Many vampaneze charged him, expecting to swat him to one side — none lived to write their memoirs.

Then, as Harkat dispatched another vampet with an almost casual swing of his axe, there was a loud, animal-like cry, and a furious R.V. entered the fray. He'd been trapped in the middle of a crowd of vampaneze, unable to join the fighting. Now at last he broke free, fixed on Harkat, and bore down upon him, hooks glinting and teeth gnashing. Tears of rage trickled from his mismatched eyes. "Kill you!" he roared. "Kill you! Kill you! Kill!"

He brought the hooks on his left hand down on

Harkat's head, but the Little Person ducked out of the way and clubbed the hooks aside with the flat of his axe. R.V. swung his other set of hooks toward Harkat's stomach. Harkat brought his free hand down in the nick of time and caught R.V.'s arm above the elbow, stopping the tips of the hooks less than an inch from the flesh of his midriff. As R.V. screamed and spat at Harkat, the Little Person calmly grabbed the straps attaching the hooks to R.V.'s arm, ripped them loose and tossed the hook-hand away.

R.V. shrieked, as though stabbed, and punched Harkat with the stump at the end of his elbow. Harkat took no notice, only reached up, caught hold of R.V.'s other hook-hand and ripped that off too.

"NO!!!" R.V. screeched, diving after the hooks. "My hands! My hands!"

R.V. recovered the hooks, but couldn't strap them back on without help. He yelled at his comrades to assist him, but they had troubles of their own. He was still screaming when Alice Burgess lowered her rifle and stared at the platform. Turning to see what she was looking at, I saw Mr. Crepsley climb over the railing, and I too relaxed.

All eyes gradually drifted to the platform and the battle died down. When people saw Mr. Crepsley standing on the platform, they stopped fighting and fixed upon the scene, sensing as I did that our squabbles were no longer relevant — the only fight that mattered was the one about to take place overhead.

When everyone was still, a strange silence settled on us, which lasted a minute or more. Mr. Crepsley stood at his end of the platform, impassive, while his three opponents stood just as sentry-like at theirs.

Finally, as the hairs on the back of my neck were beginning to lie down — they'd been standing up stiff since the start of the battle — the Lord of the Vampaneze stepped forward to the railing, lowered his hood, faced those of us on the ground, and spoke.

CHAPTER SIXTEEN

"LET THE fighting cease," the Lord of the Vampaneze said in a low, unmelodramatic voice. "There's no need for it now."

It was the first time I'd seen the Vampaneze Lord's face and I was surprised by how ordinary he looked. I'd built up a picture in my mind of a fierce, fiery, wild-eyed tyrant, whose gaze could turn water to steam. But this was just a man in his twenties or early thirties, normal build, light brown hair and rather sad eyes. The wound he'd received to his shoulder was minor — the blood had already dried — and he ignored it as he spoke.

"I knew this was coming," the Lord of the Vampaneze said softly, turning his head to gaze at Mr. Crepsley. "Des Tiny predicted it. He said I'd have to fight one of the hunters here, above the flames, and that it would most likely be Larten Crepsley. We tried to turn his prophecy on its head and lure the boy up instead. For a while I thought we'd succeeded. But in my heart I knew it was you I'd have to face."

Mr. Crepsley raised a skeptical eyebrow. "Did Mr. Tiny say which of us would triumph?" he asked.

A thin smile broke across the Vampaneze Lord's lips. "No. He said it could swing either way."

"That is encouraging," Mr. Crepsley said dryly.

Mr. Crepsley held one of his knives up to catch the light of the chandelier high above his head, studying the blade. The instant he did that, Gannen Harst stepped in front of his Lord, defensively.

"The deal's off," Harst said gruffly. "The two to one ratio no longer applies. If you'd sent Darren Shan as agreed, we'd have kept our side of the bargain. Since you've come to his place, you can't expect us to offer the same generous odds."

"I expect nothing of madmen and traitors," Mr. Crepsley said archly, causing the vampaneze and vampets in the cavern to mutter darkly.

"Take heed," Gannen Harst snarled, "or I'll —"

"Peace, Gannen," said the Lord of the Vampaneze. "The time for threats has passed. Let us lock weapons and wits without any further rancor."

The Vampaneze Lord stepped out from behind Gannen Harst and produced a barbed short sword.

Harst drew a longer, straight sword, while Steve whistled merrily and dug out a gold dagger and long length
of spiked chain.

"Are you ready, Larten Crepsley?" the Vampaneze
Lord asked. "Have you made your peace with the
gods?"

"I did that long ago," Mr. Crepsley said, both
knives in his hands, his eyes alert. "But, before we begin, I would like to know what happens after. If I win,
will my allies be set free, or must they —"

"No bargains!" the Lord of the Vampaneze
snapped. "We're not here to make deals. We're here to
fight. The fate of the others — my people and yours —
can be settled after we lock blades. Only we matter
now. All else is meaningless."

"Very well," Mr. Crepsley grunted, then stepped
away from the rail, crouched low and edged towards
his foes.

On the ground, nobody moved. Vancha, Harkat,
Debbie, Burgess and I had lowered our weapons and
were oblivious to all around us. It would have been a
simple task for the vampaneze to capture us, but they
were as captivated by events on the platform as we were.

As Mr. Crepsley advanced, the three vampaneze
assumed a "V" formation and shuffled forward a few
yards. The Vampaneze Lord was in the middle, Gannen

Harst a few feet ahead of him on his left, Steve Leopard the same distance ahead on his right. It was a cautiously effectively strategy. Mr. Crepsley would have to attack through the center — he had to kill the Vampaneze Lord; the others didn't matter. When he attacked, Harst and Steve would be able to strike from both sides at once.

Mr. Crepsley stopped short of the three, arms outstretched to protect against darting attacks from either side. His eyes were focused on the Vampaneze Lord and he didn't blink once while I was watching.

Several strained seconds passed. Then Steve lashed out at Mr. Crepsley with his chain. I saw spikes glitter as it snaked toward Mr. Crepsley's head — they'd cause serious damage if they connected. But the vampire was faster than the half-vampaneze. Twisting his head ever so slightly to the left, he avoided the chain and spikes by an inch, then stabbed sharply at Steve's stomach with the knife in his left hand.

As Mr. Crepsley attacked Steve, Gannen Harst swung at the vampire with his sword. My mouth opened to shout a warning, but then I saw I needn't bother — the vampire had been expecting the countermeasure and pivoted sweetly away from the sword, gliding inside the range of its sweep, coming within striking distance of the Vampaneze Lord.

Mr. Crepsley used the knife in his right hand to slash forward, seeking to open the Vampaneze Lord's stomach. But the leader of the vampaneze was swift and blocked the blow with his barbed sword. The tip of Mr. Crepsley's knife bit into the Lord's waist but only drew a thin trickle of blood.

Before the vampire could strike again, Steve struck at him with his dagger. He chopped wildly at Mr. Crepsley — too wild for accuracy — and forced him back. Then Gannen Harst stepped in and let fly with his sword, and Mr. Crepsley had to drop to the floor and roll backward to escape.

They were on him before he got to his feet, blades flashing, Steve's chain whipping. It took all Mr. Crepsley's speed, strength, and skill to turn the swords aside, duck out of the way of the chain, and retreat on his knees before they overwhelmed him.

As the vampaneze hastened after the vampire, I feared they had the best of him — the swords and chain were sneaking through Mr. Crepsley's desperate defenses, nicking him here, slicing him there. The wounds weren't life-threatening, but it was only a matter of time before a blade cut deeply into his stomach or chest, or the spikes of the chain snagged on his nose or eyes.

Mr. Crepsley must have known the danger he was

in, but he continued to fight a rearguard action, no longer taking the battle to the enemy, merely retreating and protecting himself as best he could, giving ground steadily, letting them push him toward the rail at the end of the platform, where he'd be cornered.

"He can't keep this up," I muttered to Vancha, who was standing close by, his eyes glued to the platform. "He's got to take a risk, and soon, before they trap him."

"You think he's unaware of that?" Vancha replied tersely.

"Then why doesn't he —"

"Hush, boy," the scruffy Prince said softly. "Larten knows what he's doing."

I wasn't so sure. Mr. Crepsley was an expert fighter, but I felt he was in over his head this time. One to one, he could handle any vampaneze. Even in a two to one situation, I'd expect him to walk away victorious. But three to one . . .

I looked for some way up to the platform — if I could join him, I might be able to turn the tide of battle. But just then, the fight took a terminal turn.

Mr. Crepsley was almost backed up against the rail, no more than two feet away from a dead end. The vampaneze knew the difficult position he was in, and

pushed forward with renewed eagerness, sensing the
end. Steve sent his chain flicking at Mr. Crepsley's face
again, for the umpteenth time, but on this occasion the
vampire didn't dodge the deadly spikes or duck out of
their way. Instead, dropping the knife in his left hand,
he reached up and grabbed the chain midair. His fingers
closed on spikes, and his mouth tightened with pain,
but he didn't let go. Yanking sharply on the chain, he
brought Steve crashing toward him. At the last possible
instant he lowered his chin, so that Steve's face connected bone-crunchingly with the vampire's forehead.

Steve's nose popped and gushed blood. He shrieked
loudly, falling to the floor. As he fell, Mr. Crepsley sent
the knife in his right hand flying at Gannen Harst, leaving himself weaponless. As Harst instinctively pulled
out of the path of the knife, the Vampaneze Lord drove
at Mr. Crepsley with his sword.

Mr. Crepsley threw himself away from the incom-
ing sword tip. Crashing into the railing, he spun
around so he was facing away from his opponents,
grabbed the rail with his hands, swung his legs and
body up with ferocious speed, and ended up doing a
handstand on the rail.

While those of us on the ground gaped, stunned
by the unexpected maneuver, Mr. Crepsley lowered

himself to chin level with the rail, then thrust away from it with all his strength. The vampire sailed, full stretch, through the air, soaring over the Vampaneze Lord and Gannen Harst — who'd stepped in front of his Lord to protect him, as he'd done many times during the fight — and Steve Leopard, who was still lying on the platform.

Mr. Crepsley landed on his feet like a cat, behind the unprotected back of the Vampaneze Lord. Before the half-vampaneze or Gannen Harst could react, Mr. Crepsley seized the Lord by the scruff of his shirt with his left hand, grabbed the waist of his trousers with his right, lifted him off the floor, spun to the edge of the platform — and tossed him head-first over the side, into the pit of stakes below!

There was time for the Lord of the Vampaneze to scream — once — then he hit the stakes with a thud which made me wince. The stakes impaled him in a dozen different places, including through the heart and head. His body twitched a couple of times, then went still, and flames caught in his hair and clothes.

It happened so fast, at first I couldn't take it all in. But as the seconds passed, and the vampaneze stared, bewildered and distraught, into the pit at the flaming corpse of their leader, the full truth struck home. Mr.

Crepsley had killed the Lord of the Vampaneze . . . without their leader, they faced destined defeat . . . the War of the Scars was over . . . the future was ours . . . we'd WON!

CHAPTER SEVENTEEN

I⟶T WAS incredible. It was almost beyond belief.

As the spirit of the vampaneze blew apart like the chains of smoke rising from their burning Lord's dead body, mine soared and I felt as though my chest would burst with relief and delight. In our darkest hour, despite the odds, against all expectations, we'd taken the fight to our foes and put their destructive designs to the sword. In my wildest dreams, I couldn't have imagined anything sweeter.

My eyes rose as Mr. Crepsley stepped to the edge of the platform. The vampire was bloodied, sweating, and exhausted, but a light shone in his eyes that could have illuminated the entire cavern. Spotting me among the shaken vampaneze, he smiled, raised a hand in salute, and opened his mouth to call something down.

That's when Steve Leopard screamed wildly and threw himself firmly into the back of the vampire.

Mr. Crepsley pitched forward, arms flailing, clutching for the rail. It looked for a split second as if he was gong to grab hold and haul himself up, but then gravity dragged him down with sickening speed, over the rail, out of safety's reach . . . into the pit after the Lord of the Vampaneze!

CHAPTER EIGHTEEN

THOUGH STEVE had sent Mr. Crepsley plummeting to his doom, he also accidentally threw the vampire a slender lifeline. Because as Mr. Crepsley toppled, Steve leaned over the railing, eager to watch the vampire hit the stakes and die. As he did, the length of chain he'd used as a weapon — which he still clutched in his right hand — unfurled and dropped beside Mr. Crepsley like a rope.

Throwing out a desperate hand, the vampire grabbed the chain, once again ignoring the pain as spikes buried themselves deep in the flesh of his palm. The chain reached its limit and snapped taut, halting Mr. Crepsley's fall.

On the platform, Steve wailed as the weight of Mr. Crepsley caused the chain to tighten around the flesh of his right hand. He tried shaking it loose, but couldn't. As he stood, leaning half over the rail, struggling with the chain, Mr. Crepsley reached up, grabbed the sleeve of Steve's shirt, and pulled him over further, caring nothing for his own life, intent only on taking Steve's.

As the pair fell — Steve screaming, Mr. Crepsley laughing — Gannen Harst thrust a hand out and caught Steve's flailing left hand. The vampaneze groaned painfully as the weight of the two men dragged on the muscles and tendons in his arm, but braced himself against an upright support post and held tight.

"Let go!" Steve screamed, kicking out at Mr. Crepsley, trying to knock him off. "You'll kill us both!"

"That is what I mean to do!" Mr. Crepsley roared. He didn't seem in the least bit bothered by the threat of death. Maybe it was the rush of adrenaline pumping through his veins, having killed the Lord of the Vampaneze — or perhaps he didn't care about his own life if it meant killing Steve. Either way, he'd accepted his fate and made no attempt to climb Steve's body to safety. In fact, he started tugging on the chain, trying to break Gannen Harst's hold.

"Stop!" Gannen Harst roared. "Stop and we'll let you go!"

"Too late!" Mr. Crepsley howled. "I swore two

things to myself when I came down here. One — I would kill the Lord of the Vampaneze. Two — I would kill Steve Leonard! I am not a man for leaving a job half done, so . . ."

He tugged even harder than before. Above him, Gannen Harst gasped and shut his eyes against the pain. "I can't . . . hold on . . . much longer!" he moaned.

"Larten!" Vancha shouted. "Don't do it! Trade your life for his. We'll track him down later and finish him off!"

"By the black blood of Harnon Oan — no!" Mr. Crepsley roared. "I have him now, so I will kill him. Let that be the end of it!"

"And what . . . about your . . . allies?" Gannen Harst shouted, and as the words penetrated Mr. Crepsley's skull, he stopped struggling and gazed up warily at the ex-protector of the Vampaneze Lord.

"As *you* hold the life of Steve Leonard in your hands," Harst said quickly, "*I* hold the lives of your friends. If you kill Steve, I'll order their deaths too!"

"No," Mr. Crepsley said quietly. "Leonard is a madman. His life must not be spared. Let me —"

"No!" Gannen Harst yelled. "Spare Steve and I'll spare the others. That's the deal. Agree to it, quick, before I lose my grip and the bloodshed continues."

Mr. Crepsley paused thoughtfully.

"His life too!" I shouted. "Spare Mr. Crepsley, or —"

"No!" Steve snarled. "Creepy Crepsley dies. I won't let him go."

"Don't be stupid!" Gannen Harst bellowed. "You'll die too if we don't release him!"

"Then I'll die," Steve sneered.

"You don't know what you're saying!" Harst hissed.

"I do," Steve replied softly. "I'll let the others go, but Crepsley dies now, because he said I was evil." Steve glared down at the silent Mr. Crepsley. "And if I have to die with him, I will — consequences be damned!"

While Gannen Harst stared at Steve, mouth agape, Mr. Crepsley looked to where Vancha and I were standing. As our eyes locked in grim understanding, Debbie rushed up beside us. "Darren!" she shouted. "We have to save him! We can't let him die! We —"

"Shhh," I whispered, kissing her forehead, holding her close.

"But —" she sobbed.

"We can't do anything," I sighed.

While Debbie moaned and buried her face in my chest, Mr. Crepsley addressed Vancha. "It seems our paths must part, Sire."

"Aye," Vancha croaked bitterly.

"We shared some good times," Mr. Crepsley said.

"Great times," Vancha corrected him.

"Will you sing my praises in the Halls of Vampire Mountain when you return, and drink a toast to me, even if it is only a glass of water?"

"I'll drink a crate of ale to your name," Vancha vowed, "and sing death songs till my voice cracks."

"You always did take things to extremes," Mr. Crepsley laughed. Then his gaze settled on me. "Darren," he said.

"Larten," I replied, smiling awkwardly. I felt like crying, but couldn't. There was an awful emptiness inside of me and my emotions wouldn't respond.

"Hurry!" Gannen Harst shouted. "My grip is slipping. A few more seconds and I'll —"

"A few seconds will suffice," Mr. Crepsley said, not one to be rushed, even when death was beckoning. Smiling sadly at me, he said, "Do not let hatred rule your life. My death does not need to be avenged. Live as a free vampire, not as a twisted, revenge-driven creature of despair. Do not become like Steve Leonard or R.V. My spirit will not rest easy in Paradise if you do."

"You don't want me to kill Steve?" I asked uncertainly.

"By all means kill him!" Mr. Crepsley boomed. "But do not devote yourself to the task. Do not —"

"I can't . . . hold . . . any longer!" Gannen Harst

wheezed. He was trembling and sweating from the strain.

"Nor shall you have to," Mr. Crepsley responded. His eyes passed from me to Vancha and back again, then up to the ceiling. He stared as though he could see through the layers of rock, concrete and earth above to the sky beyond. "Gods of the vampires!" he bellowed. "Even in death, may I be triumphant!"

Then, as the echoes of his final cry reverberated around the walls of the cavern, Mr. Crepsley let go of the chain. He hung in the air an impossible moment, almost as though he could fly . . . then dropped like a stone toward the steel-tipped stakes beneath.

CHAPTER NINETEEN

At the last possible moment, when all seemed lost, someone on a rope swung from the ceiling, streaked through the air, grabbed Mr. Crepsley around the waist, and rose with him to the safety of the platform, where they landed on their feet. As I stared, amazed, mouth hanging open, Mr. Crepsley's rescuer turned — it was Mika Ver Leth, one of my fellow Vampire Princes!

"Now!" Mika roared, and at his cry an army of vampires climbed through the holes in the ceiling and dropped to the floor, landing among the flabbergasted vampaneze and vampets. Before our foes had a chance to defend themselves, our troops were upon them, swords swinging, knives darting, axes chopping.

On the platform, Gannen Harst howled miserably — "No!" — then threw himself at Mr. Crepsley and Mika. As Harst lunged, Mika calmly stepped in front of Mr. Crepsley, drew his sword, and swung it broadly at the advancing vampaneze, cutting his head clean off at the neck, sending it sailing through the air like a misdirected bowling ball.

As Gannen Harst's lifeless, headless body toppled over the side of the platform, Steve Leopard yelped, turned, and dashed for the safety of the tunnel. He'd made it almost to the end of the plank when Mr. Crepsley borrowed one of Mika's knives, took careful aim, and sent it flashing through the air at the half-vampaneze.

The knife buried itself between Steve's shoulder blades. He gasped, stopped, spun around slowly, face white, eyes bulging, hands grasping for the hilt of the knife, unable to draw it out. Coughing up blood, he collapsed onto the plank, spasmed briefly, and fell still.

Around us, the vampires were finishing off their opponents. Harkat and Vancha had joined the fighting and were cheerfully dispatching vampaneze and vampets. Behind them, Chief Inspector Alice Burgess was gazing upon the bloodshed, unsure of who these new warriors were. She sensed they were on our side, but she held on to her rifle, just in case.

Debbie was still sobbing into my chest — she hadn't looked up and realized what was happening! "It's

OK," I told her, tilting her head up. "Mr. Crepsley's safe. He's alive. The cavalry arrived."

"*Cavalry?*" she echoed, gazing around, wiping tears from her eyes. "I don't understand. What . . . ? How . . . ?"

"I don't know!" I chortled, then grabbed Vancha's arm as he came within range. "What's going on?" I roared in his ear. "Where did this lot come from?"

"I fetched them!" he shouted gleefully. "When I left yesterday, I flitted to Vampire Mountain and told them what was going on. They flitted back with me. They had to tread cautiously — I told them not to interfere until we'd killed the Vampaneze Lord — but they've been here all along, waiting."

"But . . . I don't . . . it's . . ."

I stopped before my babbling got the better of me. I couldn't understand how they'd crept up so quietly, or how Vancha had reached Vampire Mountain and got back so quickly — even flitting, it should have taken him a few nights — but what did that matter? They were here, they were kicking butt, Mr. Crepsley was alive, and Steve Leopard and the Lord of the Vampaneze were dead. Why question it?

As I spun around like a child on Christmas Day surrounded by a room full of the most amazing presents, I saw a fabulously familiar figure pushing through the fighting, orange hair flecked with blood, a few new scars to add to the long one which carved up the left side of his face, limping on his sore ankle, but otherwise unbowed.

"Mr. Crepsley!" I roared, throwing myself into his arms.

"Master Shan!" he laughed, hugging me tight to his chest. "Did you think I was finished?"

"Yes!" I sobbed.

"Hah!" he chuckled. "You do not get rid of me that easily! You still have much to learn about our ways and customs. Who but I would have the patience to teach you?"

"Vain old geezer!" I snuffled.

"Rude young brat!" he retorted, then pushed me back to study my face. Raising a hand, he thumbed tears and dirt away from my cheeks and then . . . then . . . then . . .

CHAPTER TWENTY

No. THAT'S not how it happened.

I wish it was. With all my heart and soul, I wish he'd been rescued and our foes defeated. In that terrible, impossibly long moment of his fall, I imagined half a dozen fantastic scenarios, where Mika or Arrow or Mr. Tall intervened to divert the course of fate, and we all walked away smiling. But it wasn't to be. There was no last-minute cavalry charge. No miraculous rescue. Vancha hadn't flitted to Vampire Mountain. We were alone, as we had to be, as destiny willed it.

Mr. Crepsley dropped. He was impaled on the stakes. He died.

And it was *awful*.

I can't even say that it was quick and merciful, as it was for the Lord of the Vampaneze, because he didn't die straightaway. The stakes didn't kill him instantly, and though his soul didn't linger long, his cries while he writhed there, bleeding and dying, burning and screaming, will stay with me till I die. Maybe I'll even carry them with me when I go.

Debbie wept bitterly. Vancha howled like a wolf. Green tears trickled from Harkat's round green eyes. Even the Chief Inspector turned away from the scene and sniffed miserably.

Not me. I couldn't. My eyes stayed dry.

Stumbling forward, I stopped at the edge of the pit and stared down at the stakes and the two bodies being quickly stripped bare of their flesh by the flames. I stood as though on guard, not budging or looking away, paying no attention as the vampaneze and vampets filed silently out of the cavern. They could have executed us, but their leader was dead, their dreams had been dashed, and they were no longer interested in battle — not even in revenge.

I was barely aware of Vancha, Debbie, Harkat, and Alice Burgess as they came to stand by my side.

"We should go now," Vancha muttered after a while.

"No," I replied dully. "I'm taking him with us, to bury him properly."

"It'll be hours before the fire dies out," Vancha said.

"I'm in no rush. The hunt's over. We have all the time in the world."

Vancha sighed deeply, then nodded. "Very well. We'll wait."

"Not me," Debbie sobbed. "I can't. It's too horrible. I can't stay and . . ." She broke down in tears. I wanted to comfort her, but couldn't. There was nothing I could think to say to make her feel better.

"I'll look after her," Burgess said, taking charge. "We'll walk up the tunnel and wait for you in the smaller cavern."

"Thanks, Alice," Vancha said.

Burgess paused before leaving. "I'm still not sure about you guys," she said, "if you're really vampires or not. And I don't have a clue what I'm going to tell my people about this. But I know evil when I see it, and I like to think I know good too. I won't stand in your way when it's time for you to leave. And if you need any help, you only have to call."

"Thanks," Vancha said again, and this time he managed a thin, grateful smile.

The women left, Debbie crying, Burgess supporting her. They pushed through the departing ranks of vampaneze and vampets, who gave way meekly to the pair who'd helped bring about the downfall of their Lord.

Minutes passed. The flames flickered on. Mr. Crepsley and the Lord of the Vampaneze burned.

Then a strange-looking pair hobbled up to confront us. One had no hands, although he carried a pair of hook-hands slung around his neck. The other had only half a face and was moaning piteously. R.V. and Morgan James.

"We'll get you swine!" R.V. snarled, pointing threateningly with his left stump. "Gannen gave his word that he'd let you go, so we can't harm you now, but we'll hunt you down later and make you sorry you were born."

"You'd better come well prepared, Hooky," Vancha commented dryly. "You'll find us a real *hand*ful."

R.V. hissed at the joke and made to attack the Prince. Morgan held him back, mumbling through teeth — half of which had been shattered by Burgess' bullet — "Curhm awahy! Thuy ahn't wurth iht!"

"Hah," Vancha chuckled spitefully. "That's easy for you to say!"

This time R.V. had to push Morgan James back as he struggled to get his hands on Vancha. Cursing and fighting with each other, they backed off, joined the ranks of their numbed colleagues, and drifted away to patch themselves up and plot mean-spirited revenge.

Again we were alone at the pit. The cavern was

quieter now. Almost all the vampaneze and vampets had exited. Only a last few stragglers remained. Among them were Gannen Harst and a grinning Steve Leopard, who couldn't resist ambling over for one last mocking laugh.

"What's that cooking on the fire, boys?" he asked, putting up his hands as if to warm them.

"Go away," I said blankly, "or I'll kill you."

Steve's face dropped and he glared at me. "It's your own fault," he pouted. "If you hadn't betrayed me —"

I swung my sword up, meaning to cut him in two.

Vancha swatted it aside with the flat of his hand before I drew blood. "No," he said, stepping between us. "If you kill him, the others will return and kill us. Let it drop. We'll get him later."

"Wise words, brother," Gannen Harst said, stepping up beside Vancha. His face was drawn. "There's been enough killing. We —"

"Get lost!" Vancha snapped.

Harst's expression darkened. "Don't speak to me like —"

"I won't warn you again," Vancha growled.

The ex-protector of the Vampaneze Lord bristled angrily, then raised his hands peacefully and backed away from his brother.

Steve didn't follow.

"I want to tell him," the half-vampaneze said, eyes pinned on me.

"No!" Gannen Harst hissed. "You mustn't! Not now! You —"

"I *want* to *tell* him," Steve said again, more forcefully this time.

Harst cursed beneath his breath, glanced from one of us to the other, then nodded tensely. "Very well. But over to one side, where nobody else can hear."

"What are you up to now? Vancha asked suspiciously.

"You'll find out," Steve giggled, taking hold of my left elbow.

I shrugged him off. "Keep away from me, monster!" I spat.

"Now, now," he said. "Don't be hasty. I have news I'm bursting to tell you."

"I don't want to hear it."

"Oh, but you do," he insisted. "You'll kick yourself from here to the moon if you don't come and listen."

I wanted to tell him what he could do with his news, but there was something in his wicked eyes which made me pause. I hesitated a moment, then stomped away out of earshot of the others. Steve followed me, Gannen Harst hot on his heels.

"If you hurt him . . . ," Vancha warned them.

"We won't," Harst promised, then stopped and shielded us with his body from the view of the rest.

"Well?" I asked, as Steve stood smirking at me.

"We've come a long way, haven't we, Darren?" he remarked. "From the classroom at home to this Cavern of Retribution. From humanity to vampirism and vampanizm. From the day to the night."

"Tell me something I don't know," I grunted.

"I used to think it could have been different," he said softly, eyes distant. "But now I think it was always meant to be this way. It was your destiny to betray me and form an alliance with the vampires, your fate to become a Vampire Prince and lead the hunt for the Vampaneze Lord. Just as it was my destiny to find my own path into the night and . . ."

He stopped and a sly expression crept over his face. "Hold him," he grunted, and Gannen Harst grabbed my arms and held me rooted to the spot. "Are you ready to send him sleepy-byes?"

"Yes," Harst said. "But hurry, before the others intervene."

"Your wish is my command," Steve smiled, then put his lips close to my right ear and whispered something terrible . . . something dreadful . . . something that turned my world on its head and would haunt my every waking and sleeping moment from that instant on.

As he drew away, having tormented me with his devastating secret, I opened my mouth wide to shout the news to Vancha. Before I could utter a syllable, Gannen Harst breathed over me, the knockout gas of the vampires and vampaneze. As the fumes filled my lungs, the world around me faded, and then I was falling, unconscious, into the tortured sleep of the damned.

The last thing I heard before I blacked out was Steve, laughing hysterically — the sound of a victorious demon cackling.

CHAPTER TWENTY-ONE

I DIDN'T KNOW where I was when I awoke. I opened my eyes and saw a ceiling high above me, with lots of panels ripped out of it, three chandeliers burning dimly now that their candles were mere waxen stumps. I couldn't think where might be. I sat up, groaning, and looked for Mr. Crepsley, to ask him what was going on.

That's when I remembered.

Moaning as the painful memories returned, I clambered to my feet and looked around in desperation. The fire in the pit of stakes had almost burned itself out. Mr. Crepsley and the half-vampaneze were charred, unrecognizable collections of brittle, blackened bones. Vancha and Harkat were sitting by the edge of the pit, faces glum, silently mourning.

"How long was I out?" I shouted, lurching towards

the tunnel leading out of the cavern, falling clumsily to my knees in my frenzied haste.

"Take it easy," Vancha said, helping me back to my feet. I swiped his hands away and spun fiercely on him. *"How long?"* I roared.

Vancha eyeballed me, bemused, then shrugged. "Three hours, maybe more."

My eyelids closed hopelessly and I let myself collapse again. Too long. They'd be halfway to the other side of the world by now.

"What happened?" I asked. "The gas should have only knocked me out for fifteen or twenty minutes."

"You were exhausted," Vancha said. "It's been a long night. I'm surprised you woke this soon. It's dawn outside. We didn't expect you to stir until dusk."

I shook my head mutely, disgusted.

"Are you OK, Darren?" Harkat asked, hobbling over to join us.

"No!" I snapped. "I'm not OK. None of us is."

Rising, I brushed past the puzzled-looking pair, and made my slow, painful way to the pit, where I gazed once more upon the smoldering remains of my dearest friend and mentor.

"He's in a state of shock," I heard Vancha mutter softly to Harkat. "Go easy on him. It'll take him a while to recover."

"*Recover!*" I shrieked, sitting down and laughing maniacally.

Vancha and Harkat sat beside me, Vancha to my left, Harkat to my right. Each laid a hand on mine in a silent show of support. My throat grew tight and I thought I was going to cry at last. But after a few seconds the tears still wouldn't come, so I let my gaze drift back to the pit, while my thoughts returned to Steve's chilling revelation.

The flames grew lower and the cavern cooled. It also darkened, as the candles overhead quenched themselves one by one.

"We'd better get up there and . . . relight the candles," Harkat said, "or else we won't be able to . . . see clearly when we go down to . . . collect Mr. Crepsley's bones."

"Leave him there," I said sullenly. "This is as good a resting place as any."

Harkat and Vancha stared at me uncertainly.

"But you were the one who wanted to bury him," Vancha reminded me.

"That was before Steve took me aside," I sighed. "It doesn't matter where we leave him now. Nothing matters anymore."

"How can you say that?" Vancha snapped angrily. "We won, Darren! We killed the Lord of the

Vampaneze! The price we paid was high, but it was worth it."

"You think so?" I asked bitterly.

"Of course!" he shouted. "What's one life judged against thousands? We knew the odds coming into this. We'd have sacrificed all our lives if we had to. I feel Larten's loss as much as you — he was my friend long before he was yours. But he died honorably, and gave his life for a cause that was just. If his spirit's looking down on us, he'll be willing us to celebrate his great victory, not bemoan his —"

"You remember our first run-in with the Vampaneze Lord?" I interrupted. "You recall how he masqueraded as a servant, so we paid no notice to him and attacked the others, allowing him to escape?"

Vancha nodded warily. "Aye. What of it?"

"They tricked us then, Vancha," I said, "and they've done it again. We've won nothing. Mr. Crepsley died in vain."

Vancha and Harkat gaped at me.

"What . . . ? I don't . . . Are you saying . . . ? *What?*" Harkat gasped eventually.

"The cloaked half-vampaneze on the platform was a decoy," I sighed. "He wasn't the same person we saw in the glade. Steve told me the truth before he left. That was his parting present."

"No!" Vancha wheezed, his face ashen. "He lied! That was their Lord. The look of despair on their faces when we killed him —"

"— was genuine," I said. "Most of the vampaneze and vampets in the cavern believed he was their Lord. They were tricked just like we were. Only Gannen Harst and a handful of others knew the truth."

"Then we're back where we were at the start?" Vancha moaned. "He's alive? We've no idea what he looks like? No way of knowing where he'll turn next?"

"Not exactly," I said with a crooked half-smile. "There are only two hunters left now. That much has changed." I let out a long, disparaging breath, and gazed down into the pit again. I didn't want to tell them the rest, not coming so hot on the heels of Mr. Crepsley's death and news of the Vampaneze Lord's escape. I'd have spared them this extra blow if I could.

But they had to be warned. In case something happened to me, they had to be told, so they could spread the word and carry on without me if necessary.

"I know who he is," I whispered emotionlessly. "Steve told me. He broke the big secret. Harst didn't want him to, but he did it anyway, to hurt me that little bit more, as if Mr. Crepsley's death wasn't bad enough."

"He told you who the . . . Vampaneze Lord is?" Harkat gasped.

I nodded.

"Who?" Vancha shouted, leaping to his feet. "Which one of those scum sends others to do his dirty work for him? Tell me and I'll —"

"It's Steve," I said, and Vancha's strength deserted him. Slumping to the floor, he gazed at me in horror. Harkat too. "It's Steve," I said again, feeling empty and scared inside, knowing I'd never feel any different until — unless — he was killed, even if I lived to be a thousand. Wetting my lips, focusing on the flames, I said the whole terrible truth out loud. *"Steve Leopard is the Lord of the Vampaneze."*

After that there was only silence, burning and despair.

TO BE CONTINUED . . .

EXPLORE A NEW WORLD
AND FISH FOR THE DEAD IN

THE LAKE OF SOULS

BOOK 10 OF THE CIRQUE DU FREAK SERIES

I WAS ON THE EDGE of the camp when I spotted Mr.
Tiny and Harkat, standing in an open field. In front of
the pair stood a shimmering, arched doorway, uncon-
nected to anything else. The edges of the doorway
glowed red, and Mr. Tiny also glowed, his suit, hair
and skin a dark, vibrant, crimson shade. The space
between the edges of the doorway was a dull grey
color.

Mr. Tiny heard me coming, looked over his shoulder and smiled like a shark. "Ah — Master Shan! I
thought you might turn up."

"Darren!" Harkat snapped furiously. "I told you
not to come! I won't take you with . . . me. You'll
have to —"

Mr. Tiny laid a hand on the Little Person's back
and shoved him through the doorway. There was a

grey flash, then Harkat disappeared. I could see the field through the grey veil of the doorway — but no sign of Harkat.

"Where's he gone?" I shouted, afraid.

"To search for the truth." Mr. Tiny smiled, stepping to one side and gesturing towards the glowing doorway. "Care to search with him?"

I stepped up to the doorway, gazing uneasily at the glowing red edges and the grey sheen between. "Where does this lead?" I asked.

"Another place," Mr. Tiny answered obscurely, then laid a hand on my right shoulder and looked at me intently. "If you step through after Harkat, you might never come back. Think seriously about this. If you follow and die, you won't be here to face Steve Leonard when the time comes, and your absence might have terrible repercussions for vampires everywhere. Is your short, grey-skinned friend worth such an enormous risk?"

I didn't have to think twice about that. "Yes," I answered simply, and stepped through into unnatural, other-worldly greyness.

IF YOU'RE BLOODTHIRSTY FOR MORE, CONTINUE ON DARREN'S
SPINE-TINGLING JOURNEY WITH THE LAKE OF SOULS,
BOOK 10 OF THE CHILLING CIRQUE DU FREAK SERIES.

Book 1

CIRQUE DU FREAK
THE SAGA OF DARREN SHAN

Darren Shan is just an ordinary schoolboy—until he gets an invitation to visit the Cirque Du Freak. Soon, Darren and his friend Steve are caught in a deadly trap. Darren must make a bargain with the one person who can save Steve. But that person is not human and deals only in blood. . . .

Book 2

CIRQUE DU FREAK The Vampire's Assistant
THE SAGA OF DARREN SHAN

As a vampire's assistant, Darren struggles to resist the one temptation that sickens him—the one thing that can keep him alive. But destiny is calling—the wolf-man is waiting.

Book 3

CIRQUE DU FREAK Tunnels of Blood
THE SAGA OF DARREN SHAN

When corpses are discovered—drained of blood—Darren and Evra are compelled to hunt down whatever foul creature is committing such acts. Beneath the streets, evil stalks. Can they escape, or are they doomed to perish in the tunnels of blood?

Book 4

CIRQUE DU FREAK *Vampire Mountain*
THE SAGA OF DARREN SHAN

Darren Shan and Mr. Crepsley embark on a dangerous trek to the very heart of the vampire world. Will a meeting with the Vampire Princes restore Darren's human side, or push him further toward the darkness?

Book 5

CIRQUE DU FREAK *Trials of Death*
THE SAGA OF DARREN SHAN

Darren Shan must pass five fearsome Trials to prove himself to the vampire clan—or face the stakes in the Hall of Death. But Vampire Mountain holds hidden threats. In this nightmarish world of bloodshed and betrayal, death may be a blessing.

Book 6

CIRQUE DU FREAK *The Vampire Prince*
THE SAGA OF DARREN SHAN

Can Darren, the vampire's assistant, reverse the odds and outwit a Vampire Prince, or is this the end of thousands of years of vampire rule?

Book 7

CIRQUE DU FREAK
THE SAGA OF DARREN SHAN

Hunters of the Dusk

As part of an elite force, Darren searches the world for the Vampaneze Lord. But the road ahead is long and dangerous — and lined with the bodies of the damned.

Book 8

CIRQUE DU FREAK
THE SAGA OF DARREN SHAN

Allies of the Night

Darren Shan, Vampire Prince and vampaneze killer, faces his worst nightmare yet — school! But homework is the least of Darren's problems. Bodies are piling up. Time is running out.

Book 10

CIRQUE DU FREAK
THE SAGA OF DARREN SHAN

The Lake of Souls

Darren and Harkat face monstrous obstacles on their desperate quest to the Lake of Souls. Will they survive the savage journey? And what awaits them in the murky waters of the dead? Be careful what you fish for. . . .

CIRQUE DU FREAK
THE SAGA OF DARREN SHAN

Lord of the Shadows

Darren Shan is going home—and his world is going to hell. Old enemies await. Scores must be settled. Destiny looks certain to destroy him, and the world is set to fall to the Ruler of the Night....

CIRQUE DU FREAK
THE SAGA OF DARREN SHAN

Sons of Destiny

The time has finally come for Darren to face his archenemy, Steve Leopard. One of them will die. The other will become the Lord of the Shadows—and destroy the world. Is the future written or can Darren trick destiny?

Grubbs Grady is about to learn three things:
The world is vicious. Magic is possible.
Demons are real.

Turn the page for a sneak peek at Darren Shan's
bloodcurdling new novel:

LORD LOSS

Book 1 in the DEMONATA series

Available now.

✠ Purgatory. Confined to my room after school for a month. A whole bloody *MONTH*! No TV, no computer, no comics, no books — except schoolbooks. Dad leaves my chess set in the room too — no fear my chess-crazy parents would take *that* away from me! Chess is almost a religion in this house. My sister Gret and I were reared on it. While other toddlers were being taught how to put jigsaws together, we were busy learning the ridiculous rules of chess.

I can come downstairs for meals, and bathroom visits are allowed, but otherwise I'm a prisoner. I can't even go out on the weekends.

In solitude, I call Gret every name under the moon the first night. Mom and Dad bear the brunt of my curses the next. After that I'm too miserable to blame anyone, so I sulk in moody silence and play chess against myself to pass the time.

They don't talk to me at meals. The three of them act like I'm not not there. Gret doesn't even glance at me spitefully and sneer, the way she usually does when I'm getting the doghouse treatment.

But what have I done that's so bad? OK, it was a crude joke and I knew I'd get into trouble — but their reactions are waaaaaaay over the top. If I'd done something to embarrass Gret in public, fair enough, I'd take what was coming. But this was a private joke, just between us. They shouldn't be making such a song and dance about it.

Dad's words echo back to me — "And the timing!" I think about them a lot. And Mom's, when she was going at me about smoking, just before Dad cut her short — "We don't need this, certainly not at this time, not when —"

What did they mean? What were they talking about? What does the timing have to do with anything?

Something stinks here — and it's not just rat guts.

✚ I spend a lot of time writing. Diary entries, stories, poems. I try drawing a comic — "Grubbs Grady, Superhero!" — but I'm no good at art. I get great marks in my other subjects — way better than goat-faced Gret ever gets, as I often remind her — but I've got all the artistic talent of a duck.

I play lots of games of chess. Mom and Dad are chess fanatics. There's a board in every room and they play several games most nights, against each other or friends from their chess clubs. They make Gret and me play too. My earliest memory is of sucking on a white rook while Dad explained how a knight moves.

I can beat just about anyone my age — I've won

regional competitions — but I'm not in the same class as Mom, Dad, or Gret. Gret's won at national level and can wipe the floor with me nine times out of ten. I've only ever beaten Mom twice in my life. Dad — never.

It's been the biggest argument starter all my life. Mom and Dad don't put pressure on me to do well in school or at other games, but they press me all the time at chess. They make me read chess books and watch videotaped tournaments. We have long debates over meals and in Dad's study about legendary games and grandmasters, and how I can improve. They send me to tutors and keep entering me in competitions. I've argued with them about it — I'd rather spend my time watching and playing basketball — but they've always stood firm.

White rook takes black pawn, threatens black queen. Black queen moves to safety. I chase her with my bishop. Black queen moves again — still in danger. This is childish stuff — I could have cut off the threat five moves back, when it became apparent — but I don't care. In a petty way, this is me striking back. "You take my TV and computer away? Stick me up here on my own? OK — I'm gonna learn to play the worst game of chess in the world. See how you like that, Corporal Dad and Commandant Mom!"

Not exactly Luke Skywalker striking back against the evil Empire by blowing up the *Death Star*, I know, but hey, we've all gotta start somewhere!

✠ Studying my hair in the mirror. Stiff, tight, ginger. Dad used to be ginger when he was younger, before the grey set in. Says he was fifteen or sixteen when he noticed the change. So, if I follow in his footprints, I've only got a handful or so years of unbroken ginger to look forward to.

I like the idea of a few grey hairs, not a whole head of them like Dad, just a few. And spread out — I don't want a skunk patch. I'm big for my age — taller than most of my friends — and burly. I don't look old, but if I had a few grey hairs, I might be able to pass for an adult in poor light — bluff my way into R-rated movies!

The door opens. Gret — smiling shyly. I'm nineteen days into my sentence. Full of hate for Gretelda Grotesque. She's the last person I want to see.

"Get out!"

"I came to make up," she says.

"Too late," I snarl nastily. "I've only got eleven days to go. I'd rather see them out than kiss your . . ." I stop. She's holding out a plastic bag. Something blue inside. "What's that?" I ask suspiciously.

"A present to make up for getting you grounded," she says, and lays it on my bed. She glances out of the window. The curtains are open. A three-quarters moon lights up the sill. There are some chess pieces on it, from when I was playing earlier. Gret shivers, then turns away.

"Mom and Dad said you can come out — the punishment's over. They've ended it early."

She leaves.

Bewildered, I tear open the plastic. Inside — a New York Knicks jersey, shorts and socks. I'm stunned. The Knicks are my team, my basketball champions. Mom used to buy me their latest gear at the start of every season, until I hit puberty and sprouted. She won't buy me any new gear until I stop growing — I outgrew the last one in just a month.

This must have cost Gret a fortune — it's brand new, not last season's. This is the first time she's ever given me a present, except at Christmas and birthdays. And Mom and Dad have never cut short a grounding before — they're very strict about making us stick to any punishment they set.

What the hell is going on?

✠ Three days after my early release. To say things are strange is the understatement of the decade. The atmosphere's just like it was when Grandma died. Mom and Dad wander around like robots, not saying much. Gret mopes in her room or in the kitchen, stuffing herself with sweets and playing chess non-stop. She's like an addict. It's bizarre.

I want to ask them about it, but how? "Mom, Dad — have aliens taken over your bodies? Is somebody dead and you're too afraid to tell me? Have you all converted to Miseryism?"

Seriously, jokes aside, I'm frightened. They're sharing a secret, something bad, and keeping me out of it. Why? Is it to do with me? Do they know something that I don't? Like maybe . . . maybe . . .

(Go on — have the guts! Say it!)

Like maybe *I'm* going to die?

Stupid? An overreaction? Reading too much into it? Perhaps. But they cut short my punishment. Gret gave me a present. They look like they're about to burst into tears at any given minute.

Grubbs Grady — on his way out? A deadly disease I caught on vacation? A brain defect that I've had since birth? The big, bad Cancer bug?

What other explanation is there?

✤ "Regale me with your thoughts on ballet."

I'm watching basketball highlights. Alone in the TV room with Dad. I cock my ear at the weird, out-of-nowhere question and shrug. "Rubbish," I snort.

"You don't think it's an incredibly beautiful art form? You've never wished to experience it first-hand? You don't want to glide across Swan Lake or get sweet with a Nutcracker?"

I choke on a laugh. "Is this a windup?"

Dad smiles. "Just wanted to check. I got a great offer on tickets to a performance tomorrow. I bought three — anticipating your less-than-enthusiastic reaction — but I could probably get an extra one if you want to tag along."

"No way!"

"Your loss." Dad clears his throat. "The ballet's out of town and finishes quite late. It will be easier for us to stay in a hotel overnight."

"Does that mean I'll have the house to myself?" I ask excitedly.

"No such luck," he chuckles. "I think you're old enough to guard the fort, but Sharon" — Mom — "has a different view, and she's the boss. You'll have to stay with Aunt Kate."

"Not no-date Kate," I groan. Aunt Kate's only a couple of years older than Mom, but lives like a nine-ty-year-old. Has a black-and-white TV but only turns it on for the news. Listens to radio the rest of the time. "Couldn't I kill myself instead?" I quip.

"Don't make jokes like that!" Dad snaps with unexpected venom. I stare at him, hurt, and he forces a thin smile. "Sorry. Hard day at the office. I'll arrange it with Kate, then."

He stumbles as he exits — as if he's nervous. For a minute there it was like normal, me and Dad messing around, and I forgot all my recent worries. Now they come flooding back. If I'm not at death's door, why was he so upset at my throwaway gag?

Curious and afraid, I slink to the door and eavesdrop as he phones Aunt Kate and clears my stay with her. Nothing suspicious in their conversation. He doesn't talk about me as if these are my final days. Even hangs up with a cheery "Toodle-oo," a corny phrase he often uses on the phone. I'm about to withdraw and catch up with the basketball action when I hear Gret speaking softly from the stairs.

"He didn't want to come?"

"No," Dad whispers back.

"It's all set?"

"Yes. He'll stay with Kate. It'll just be the three of us."

"Couldn't we wait until next month?"

"Best to do it now — it's too dangerous to put off."

"I'm scared, Dad."

"I know, love. So am I."

Silence.

✣ Mom drops me off at Aunt Kate's. They exchange some small talk on the doorstep, but Mom's in a rush and cuts the conversation short. Says she has to hurry or they'll be late for the ballet. Aunt Kate buys that, but I've cracked their cover story. I don't know what Mom and Co. are up to tonight, but they're not going to watch a load of poseurs in tights jumping around like puppets.

"Be good for your aunt," Mom says, tweaking the hairs on my forehead.

"Enjoy the ballet," I reply, smiling hollowly.

Mom hugs me, then kisses me. I can't remember the last time she kissed me. There's something desperate about it.

"I love you, Grubitsch!" she croaks, almost sobbing.

If I hadn't already known something was very, very wrong, the dread in her voice would have tipped me off. Prepared for it, I'm able to grin and flip back at her, Humphrey Bogart style, "Love you too, shweetheart."

Mom drives away. I think she's crying.

"Make yourself comfy in the living room," Aunt Kate simpers. "I'll fix a nice pot of tea for us. It's almost time for the news."

I make an excuse after the news. Sore stomach — need to rest. Aunt Kate makes me gulp down two large spoons of cod liver oil, then sends me up to bed.

I wait five minutes, until I hear Frank Sinatra crooning — no-date Kate loves Ol' Blue Eyes and always manages to find him on the radio. When I hear her singing along to some corny ballad, I slip downstairs and out the front door.

I don't know what's going on, but now that I know I'm not set to go toes-up, I'm determined to see it through with them. I don't care what sort of a mess they're in. I won't let Mom, Dad, and Gret freeze me out, no matter how bad it is. We're a family. We should face things together. That's what Mom and Dad always taught me.

Padding through the streets, covering the four miles home as quickly as I can. They could be anywhere, but I'll start with the house. If I don't find them there, I'll look for clues to where they might be.

I think of Dad saying he's scared. Mom trembling as she kissed me. Gret's voice when she was on the stairs. My stomach tightens with fear. I ignore it, jog at a steady pace, and try spitting the taste of cod liver oil out of my mouth.

✠ Home. I spot a chink of light in Mom and Dad's bedroom, where the curtains just fail to meet. It doesn't mean they're in — Mom always leaves a light on to deter burglars. I slip around the back and peer through the garage window. The car's parked inside. So they're here. This is where it all kicks off. Whatever "it" is.

I creep up to the back door. Crouch, poke the dog flap open, listen for sounds. None. I was eight when our last dog died. Mom said she was never allowing another one inside the house — they always got killed on the roads and she was sick of burying them. Every few months, Dad says he must board over the dog flap or get a new door, but he never has. I think he's still secretly hoping she'll change her mind. Dad loves dogs.

When I was a baby, I could crawl through the flap. Mom had to keep me tied to the kitchen table to stop me from sneaking out of the house when she wasn't looking. Much too big for it now, so I fish under the pyramid-shaped stone to the left of the door and locate the spare key.

The kitchen's cold. It shouldn't be — the sun's been shining all day and it's a nice warm night — but it's like standing in a refrigerator aisle in a supermarket.

I creep to the hall door and stop, again listening for sounds. None.

Leaving the kitchen, I check the TV room, Mom's fancily decorated living room — off-limits to Gret and me except on special occasions — and Dad's study. Empty. All as cold as the kitchen.

Coming out of the study, I notice something strange and do a double-take. There's a chess board in one corner. Dad's prize chess set. The pieces are based on characters from the King Arthur legends. Hand-carved by some famous craftsman in the nineteenth century. Cost a fortune. Dad never told Mom the exact price — never dared.

I walk to the board. Carved out of marble, four inches thick. I played a game with Dad on its smooth surface just a few weeks ago. Now it's rent with deep, ugly gouges. Almost like fingernail scratches — except no human could drag their nails through solid marble. And all the carefully crafted pieces are missing. The board's bare.

Up the stairs. Sweating nervously. Fingers clenched tight. My breath comes out as mist before my eyes.

Part of me wants to turn tail and run. I shouldn't be here. I don't *need* to be here. Nobody would know if I backed up and . . .

I flash back to Gret's face after the rat guts prank. Her tears. Her pain. Her smile when she gave me the Knicks jersey. We fight all the time, but I love her deep down. And not that deep either.

I'm not going to leave her alone with Mom and Dad to face whatever trouble they're in. Like I told myself earlier — we're a family. Dad's always said families should pull together and fight as a team. I want to be part of this — even though I don't know what "this" is, even though Mom and Dad did all they could to keep me out of "this," even though "this" terrifies me senseless.

The landing. Not as cold as downstairs. I try my bedroom, then Gret's. Empty. Very warm. The chess pieces on Gret's board are also missing. Mine haven't been taken, but they lie scattered on the floor and my board has been smashed to splinters.

I edge closer to Mom and Dad's room. I've known all along that this is where they must be. Delaying the moment of truth. Gret likes to call me a coward when she wants to hurt me. Big as I am, I've always gone out of my way to avoid fights. I used to think (*fear*) she might be right. Each step I take towards my parents' bedroom proves to my surprise that she was wrong.

The door feels red hot, as though a fire is burning behind it. I press an ear to the wood — if I hear the crackle of flames, I'll race straight to the phone and dial 911. But there's no crackle. No smoke. Just deep, heavy breathing . . . and a curious dripping sound.

My hand's on the doorknob. My fingers won't move. I keep my ear pressed to the wood, waiting . . . praying. A tear trickles from my left eye. It dries on my cheek from the heat.

Inside the room, somebody giggles — low, throaty, sadistic. Not Mom, Dad, or Gret. There's a ripping sound, followed by snaps and crunches.

My hand turns.

The door opens.

Hell is revealed.

What evil does Grubbs find behind the door?

Read all of **LORD LOSS**, Book 1 in the DEMONATA series, available now.

The Demonata exist in a multi-world universe of their own.
Evil, murderous creatures who revel in torment and slaughter.
They try to cross over into our world all the time.

Don't miss Darren Shan's
chilling DEMONATA series.

And watch out for *Blood Beast*,
coming October 2007.